BETWEEN FAMILIES

D1738650

Karin Mitchell

ISBN: 1499584776
ISBN 13: 9781499584776
Library of Congress Control Number: **2014920980**
CreateSpace Independent Publishing Platform
North Charleston, South Carolina

ACKNOWLEDGEMENTS

Before bed last night, less than 2 weeks before the release of this novel, my four-year-old wanted to know what I wished on the stars for. I equivocated saying I wasn't sure if I was supposed to share what I wish for. He said, "daddy always tells me he wishes that people will read your book and that they'll like your book." I cried, of course. That much love and support ... well... I'm lucky is all.

So I have to thank my husband, Rob. Without his quiet, music-soul, I wouldn't have written. At least, not like this. He always lets me go and takes care of the kids when I need to get out and ski or write and I can't imagine anyone I'd rather parent with or navigate all the ups and downs of life. And dang, if writing doesn't have some ups and downs. He's steady though. He somehow never says the wrong thing and really *gets* it. My husband and the family we've created are the ground from which I step into the world and I'm profoundly grateful for that. Plus, he's kind of a looker;)

To my family for being a whole lotta awesome. From my dad who I have to talk to about every single life decision, to my in-laws who bragged about me when I was a slacker-ski bum, to my brother who is so meticulous, I can't imagine how to write without someone like him in my back pocket, to my mom, whew, what to say about her? She's pretty much the nicest person in the world. She gives Christians a good name—she'd really give you the shirt off her back, no judgments. Without her this book wouldn't exist. For all the times she took my kids because they hadn't let me sleep a wink or so I could write or ski or fold laundry. She was my biggest champion during the Kickstarter campaign. She's just always in my corner.

But before, or in front of, or beyond that, my parents said "yes." They said, "you can." They taught me I was smart and could do anything. Despite a colorful childhood, they delivered the most important message of all: I am loved and valuable.

To all the people who read the first shitty draft of this novel and didn't say it sucked. For all the people who read subsequent drafts and weren't afraid to tell me what was wrong because it helped shape it into something better.

Thank to Elisabeth Kinsey who painstakingly went through the first draft and helped me tease out the book from the slush.

To my editor, Laura K. Anderson who has believed in the project and held my hand while also editing with the vigor and ruthlessness that such pursuit requires. Thank god for you! May you achieve all the success you deserve and still charge me the pittance you do. Your belief in this project has meant the world to me, especially because I know you to be scrupulous and discerning and always striving for correctness!

To Michael O'Donnell who helped me during my crisis of finding that I have faith and who also helped with the proofreading.

To Erica Currey and Rocky Mountain Montessori for being a safe place where my kids are loved and well-looked after so that I can dismiss them from my mind while I write this difficult subject-matter and protect their souls from the darkness of the world for a little longer. You're wonderful. I'm truly grateful for the trust I'm able to place in my high-quality providers. I wish I could pay you the moon.

To Melanie Rippetoe for being the first person I ever shared my writing with.

To Amber Brummer for creating my Kickstarter video and doing way above and beyond what I deserved with the material I gave her to work with. Seriously, I made weird faces a lot during the filming of that video. I'm sure of it.

To Harrison Fletcher for giving me that one B+. Because nothing is at once more frustrating and motivating as a B+. I worked harder.

To all the professors who were critically encouraging.

To my high school English teacher, at Parkway North in Creve Coeur, MO, Dr. Eichhorn. You read to us and with us and taught me that books can be art. You showed me Toni Morrison and painstakingly taught me what she meant. Someday I hope I hope to make art that stops your breath, that you have to swallow down like a key, forcing its way to your heart through the constricted space of your throat.

Thank you to all the places where I wrote, edited, rewrote, edited some more, and conceived this: A Basin, the Silverthorne Library, the Pour house, Tennyson Center for Children, and more. Thank you to all the artists whose works have nurtured creativity and healing in me.

To Magnus, Lotta, and Joel Wretblad. Who knew I had even more family in Sweden? Joel is the baby brother I was meant to get but just had to wait until he was a 17-year-old exchange student. And his parents have been as huge in championing this book as my own parents. Magnus is responsible for the beautiful cover you see pictured.

Thank you to Diane Pocius and Gina Sheridan for helping me get into grad school. Without working on my writing in that arena, it wouldn't be where it is today.

To the low-cost conferences I attended during the making of this book that helped me stay motivated and gave me practical suggestions and contacts: Tallgrass Writer's Workshop and NW Women's Small Business Conference.

Special thanks to the wonderful coworkers I've had over the years which are too numerous to mention here and have cared so much for the kids who really needed them. I've known at least a hundred people in my lifetime who were truly great human beings; who took the time to try their best to bring their gifts and talents to kids, and not the easy kids. The kids who make you work for it. You are who this is truly for. Thanks for making me work for it. I hope it helps.

KICKSTARTER

To everyone who supported the Kickstarter campaign to get enough money to bring this project to fruition. Thank you.

The fundraising effort was epic. It was difficult and humbling and frustrating and exhilarating and scary. It helped me hone my message in conveying to others what this book is about and why they should give a shit. The involvement of all of you in believing in the project and sharing it with others, donating, and talking about it has helped push Between Families forward. It showed me how I was alone in making this into a reality. Thank you especially to Michelle Woods Pennisi. She donated $1300 worth of ceramics to be sold to support the Kickstarter and helped me get together an in person fundraiser in 10 days. Thank you to Bryan Dean, owner of the Pour House, who encouraged us to use his venue to host the event. He even got Noodles & Co to donate food. Thank you to Josiah Hutchinson who volunteered his time to work the event and to Marci Perot who took care of the kids so we could attend. Thank you to my mom, dad, and husband who worked their butts off at the event, convincing people to do Mad Libs and donate money. And thank you to my sister-in-law who encouraged me to wear a necklace that said "Dope." Because, when it's your event, you should wear a ridiculous outfit including a diamond patterned miniskirt and a gold pendant.

Thank you to all the people who attended the In Person Event: Artists Helping Artists.

Thank you to the following people who backed the Kickstarter campaign online:
*Amber Sansaver Scott *Alli Gober *Andy P. Bullen *Angela Carosello *Anna Tekla Prescott *Anne Kluesner *Barbara Brooks *Becky Falch *Bradley Pennington *Brian Foss *Carley Margolis Taylor *Bryan Dean- The Pour House *Caroline Breton *Clara Lyford *Daniel Prescott *Deanna Balestra *Deborah Price *Donna Freda *Eric Schmidt *Elliot Kwiatkowski *Elizabeth Swaggerty *George A Mitchell *Janet Fenton *Jason Gould *Jean McArthur *Jim, Kate, Collin, and Darren Brown *Joel Wretblad *Joni Bauer *Josh Flenniken *Jorja Beert *Julie Hutson *Julie Wolfington *Katie Murphy *Kelley Anne *Kevin Burns *Kurt Baehmann *Lenka Lesmerises *Marcus and Teresa Jackson *Marsha A Harvey*Magnus Wretblad *Matt Obermeier *Matt Cox *Meghann Mohan *Melanie Rippetoe *Michelle Woods Pennisi *Mike D *Misty Stieber *Natalie Gibson *Rachel and Ben Treiger *Rhonda Bird *Ruth Hendricks*Sabrina Lunn *Sarah Hester *Shannon Farrell *Shannon Quinn *Shannon, JJ, Case, Dirk, and Reece *Sammy Charytoniuk *Scott Sperry *Tom Klezker *Thomas Arvidsson *Tracy Ma *Wendy D'Ottavio *Zina Bauman

Kickstarter: 140 Character notes promised to backers who donated at a level of $50 or higher
Caroline Breton- This masterpiece has been in the making forever and looking forward to reading it again

Marsha A Harvey- Watching your writing develop has been a joy. Your talent and efforts show in this book. Congratulations.
George A Mitchell- Thanks for a wonderfully powerful work, written with love and sincerity.

ON CONTENT

Trigger warning:** Victims of sexual assault and especially victims of childhood molestation and sexual abuse should be warned that this book contains graphic descriptions.

Between Families takes place in the nineties in St. Louis and the surrounding areas. I want to clarify that residential treatment centers often did restrain children at that point for noncompliance (not doing what they were told.) They no longer do this. Policies have changed significantly since then. Children are no longer permitted to nap after a restraint and good facilities only put their hands on children in the most extreme instances where safety is at issue. The book is intended to show the reality of these places, and many of the scenes are as true today as they were then. Some things are different now, though.

The character, Seffra, comments in this book that teachers in RTCs "still thought school was important; they seemed less consumed by the importance of their subjects. They seemed to recognize that in our lives there were other things going on. Or maybe they were just bad teachers." I want to say that I have met a lot of great teachers in RTCs, and this was meant as a comment from the perspective of a child.

Seffra Morgan is a fictional character, built to tell us a truth about our world in a way that only fiction can. She is a composite based on real children. I chose to tell the story of kids in treatment with a fictional character in order to keep the stories of the kids I knew intact. Should they wish to tell their own truth in writing, I enthusiastically encourage them to do so. The door is open.

As a special education teacher I worked in residential treatment as well as public schools. I went on to do work in child welfare for a brief time. In all that time, I discovered that children, once removed from their homes, sometimes do NOT go to foster care.

CHILDREN! I don't know about you, but there was nothing more important to my childhood than being cared for by parents. The idea that the reality for many children in this country is a life in an institution where they get hugs that do not involve full body contact and squeezing haunts me to this day. It should haunt you too. For kids who live this reality, I hope this story helps you understand yourself better. I know it helped me to put myself in your shoes. Your shoes are huge and hard to walk around in, and you possess a wealth of skills and abilities that have helped you navigate the world. Don't let anybody tell you that you can't.

Still, Seffra is one character. She cannot represent the over 200,000 children currently living in institutions. Please understand that I included the character Danny specifically to represent the disproportionate number of children in care who have cognitive disabilities. They are at greater risk for all manner of mistreatment and tend to be less resilient in recovering. They are more likely to age out and in the long term and end up homeless. The character who was a prostitute is also based on a real girl. Do not be naive. This happens in our country, in our communities, and to children far younger than Seffra. This was the only thing I could think to do to advocate for these voiceless children.

I humbly offer this book and hope it helps.

In Gracious Memory of the Life and Work of David Ramos

BETWEEN FAMILIES

Karin Mitchell

Part I:
Darkness and Love

1

Between the last dry grains of sand and the first drops of sea. Between the sun's last sliver of light slipping below the horizon and the stars' first winks. Between the last scenes in dreams and wiping sleep from weary eyes, therein lies the truth.

The truth lies in between.

Between the story you tell and the one your mother tells. Between what a murderer remembers and what a witness speaks. Between being yanked out of the messy life you were born into and piecing together a new one from the scraps you beg, borrow, and steal. That's where the truth is and where the story lies: in between. Beginnings and endings are arbitrary. My story could start with my parents.

He shot her in the face. When my mother was eight months pregnant with me, my mother and father were up late fighting in their shabby, one-bedroom apartment when my father held a gun to her cheek and pulled the trigger. She heard the barrel click, and quickly jerked her head up and over. So the bullet didn't blast through her skull and kill her. It didn't split us apart. Instead, it sliced a fine path up the bridge of her nose. It narrowly missed her eye, singeing eyelashes on its way up her face, scraping her just beneath her right eyebrow and lodging itself in the wall behind her. But she was fine. And I was fine. He must've been a fucking horrible shot.

There were only two signs my mom'd been shot and neither of them noticeable. One was that she had no sense of smell. If a skunk came through and sprayed, she'd be blissfully unaware. She also had a slender scar, barely there, that ran up the bridge of her nose to her eyebrow. That was it. My mom was rarely seen without her stylish sunglasses and a layer of glossy lipstick. She had lustrous red hair, very light skin and full lips, and the combination meant you only saw the scar if you knew what you were looking for. She was beautiful.

I remember sitting in our kitchen staring at the white plaster wall and wondering about that bullet. I always pictured the shooting in our apartment, even though it hadn't taken place there.

I imagined my mom's refusal to give in, even with a gun to her face. People thought my mother was smooth and sultry and she was. She dripped southern charm and men lapped it up. But beneath all that sweetness was a stubborn woman who was tough as nails and who couldn't be told what to do.

The thick, sun-dried knuckles of my father's left hand grasped my mom's untamed hair while he held a gun to her face with his right. She looked up and stared right into his face. Unflinchingly she held his gaze and goaded him to *do it*. When he didn't right away, she told him to fuck himself. So he shot her.

Covered in blood at the hospital, they told her she and the baby were both fine. I'm sure they told her how lucky she'd been. How lucky we'd both been. All she knew was she'd done what she had to in order to keep me with her. She stood up to that son of a bitch and she kept us together.

My dad went to jail for trying to kill my mom. I never met him; he was already in jail when I was born. But I imagined the story often. Especially two parts of the story: the shooting, and right after when my mom lay in her hospital bed in Georgia.

Crisp, clean sheets tucked neatly around the metal rails of a bed and the nurses and the doctors fussing over us and saying how lucky we'd been. A kind nurse would gently touch my mother's rounded belly.

"We're fine," my mother would say firmly.

And my mother would glare and wish her hands away. Because she'd been the one who'd protected us from him.

She'd touch the bandage on her face and say, "I did what I had to."

She could have done nothing. She kept us together for 12 years. It could have been worse.

"You're very lucky. This could have been much worse," I imagined them telling her.

They told me the same thing when I fractured my skull.

"Seffra, this could have been much, much worse. You're very lucky."

I was six and playing with Neil Crosby, my best friend's older brother, who was trying to figure out how to bat left-handed. I shuffled my feet around, trying to find the right spot in the dust of the baseball diamond at the elementary school across the street. I'd chosen my spot wrong, thinking he'd swing right-handed. I hadn't understood the bat could come from the other direction. He tossed the white ball up into the bright hot blue sky and we both watched it go up and up and then come down fast. Before I knew it, the ball was there, and he swung wildly. I don't know if he made contact with the ball, but he sure made contact with my head.

I drove everyone crazy, crying and rocking with my head in my hands, asking over and over again for my mom. I couldn't remember what had happened from one moment to the next. The Crosbys waited and waited for my mom to come home from wherever she was, but after hours of waiting and worrying, they finally gave up and took me to the emergency room. When I was home after the initial ordeal, Neil's mom came by and scolded my mother for not being home on time. She knocked on the door while I was on the couch resting, still in pain.

"You should've left us a number at least, Lindy. What were you thinking?"

The woman whispered all the details at my mom and you could hear the scolding in her tone.

My mom didn't *do* scolding, not even from Mrs. Crosby.

"I'll thank y' kindly to keep y'opinions to y'self. Have a nice day." She said too-sweetly and slammed the door in the woman's face. We stopped talking to them after that and I wasn't allowed to play at the Crosby's until long after their mother died in a drunk driving accident. It was their father who was the drunk driver. Imagine that. Their mom died and their dad went to jail for driving drunk with her in the car. My mom had been involved in the incident, too. She should've been the one driving, actually, but I didn't learn all that until I came to live with the Crosby's and got thrown out of the house.

At the hospital, they checked me out and then sent me home with orders to follow up with a doctor the next day. I don't know who they thought the neighbors were. I don't remember much from that day. The first thing I remember after the sun and the baseball was waking up in the early hours of the morning with a searing pain that seemed to extend beyond the size of what could possibly be my head. I sat straight up, smelling my mom's perfume and sugary sour-breath and realized it was her fluffy comforter I was sweating under, the thick one with the big pink roses in full bloom.

"What happened?" I whined. Sweat glued my unruly hair to my forehead and was certainly weaving a massive rat's nest at the base of my skull.

"Aw, Seffra baby, not again. I keep tellin' you doll, you hit y' head." Pale light streaked through the dusty blinds and she stroked back the hair off my sticky forehead. I looked at the familiar pink rose wallpaper border that matched my mother's bedspread and tried to nestle into the comfort, but I couldn't get comfortable; it hurt too much.

"I did?" I reached my hand up and felt the gravel still on my forehead but I didn't know why it was there. I couldn't put the baseball diamond together with what she told me. The sunny sky was a lifetime ago. There was only the clear pain pushing its size outward and the big rosy bed.

"I've told you over and over." Her brow scrunched down low. She wasn't wearing any glasses or eye make-up. Her scar exposed, she looked tired.

Later that day, my mom actually drove me to the doctor. She borrowed her boyfriend-at-the time's Cadillac to take me. She was sober and completely focused on me. It was glorious, even with the pain.

She didn't say "God dammit, Seffra!" when I whined and cried every time the car bounced over a crack in the concrete. It hurt so bad. She didn't get mad even when I threw up out the window and vomit slid down side of the newly-washed white door.

Instead, she said, "I'm so sorry, baby," and ran her hand along my hair, telling me I was going to be okay. She listened to the doctor and asked questions about whether I'd have permanent damage and what she needed to do to take care of me.

The doctor told us the story of Phineas Gage. In 1848 there was this guy who took a three-foot rod through the head. The thing was an inch and a quarter in diameter. He was a foreman working on the railroad, and there was an explosion that sent this iron rod rocketing through the air, passing through his skull on its way. The guy was fine.

He twitched a little, stood up, and was clear-headed as always. The only thing different about Mr. Phin after his accident was that he went from being a straight-laced, run-of- the-mill nice guy, to a loose-lipped, sailor slush-mouth so full of shit that no one who hadn't seen it for themselves believed his story about the rod skewering his head.

They just thought he was always an asshole.

The doctor explained how head injuries are each so different: some people walk away perfectly aware and fine. (My mom had, but he didn't know that.) And maybe ol' Phineas had been looking out for me. (Maybe Phineas had been looking out for me for a long time.) The doctor probably didn't mean it as literally as I took it.

I never was much for God, but I totally believed in the possibility of ghosts. Good and bad ones. So I believed what the doctor said was true: that Phineas had been there for my head wound and had watched over me. The doctor also explained how Phineas became a lying miscreant afterwards. So sometimes I thought of Phineas as a mean ghost to pin the blame on. Whether he was watching out for me, or I was blaming him for something, when I talked to him I called him Uncle Phin.

Like when I poured my mom's whiskey down the drain. *What do I do, Uncle Phin? Any ideas?*

That's when I got the itch to dump it. I hated when my mom drank and used to think that if I could get rid of the alcohol in the house she'd stop drinking and be nice again. I risked getting caught and being in big trouble for it, but usually if I did dump it, she'd think she drank it all or that one of her friends did it at the last party. But sometimes she figured it was me, and she'd slap me over and over and tell me to "stay outa my things, wretched girl!"

Thanks a lot, Uncle Phin, I'd think, blaming him. He was the one who'd convinced me to pour the whiskey out, but then where was he when the blame came crashing down around my face?

Other times I felt guilty for blaming him and knew with absolute certainty that he was a guardian angel watching over me.

"You're very lucky, Seffra. This could have been much worse." I imagined Uncle Phin comforting me with this phrase when my mom went missing and I was hungry. I'd have eaten all the food in the house already. She'd be gone for days and I'd be staying in the apartment waiting for her to get back, hoping she'd be bringing food when she came and thinking how it could have been worse if she had left me with no food at all, and listening to Uncle Phin telling me that she'd be home soon.

꩜

I don't know for a fact that it changed her demeanor at all, getting shot, I mean, but after I heard about Phineas Gage, I believed that a perfect, nice-mommy was stuck in my mom that her bullet trapped inside. I'd picture Uncle Phin as a ghost or a guardian head-injury angel, watching over us, trying to help my mom be nice, and keeping us together.

There were times when I caught a glimpse of the nice-mommy I believed was my real mom, like when she took care of me after my head injury, and in those glimpses it was like having a movie star for a mom. She was fashionable. She was exciting. She was beautiful and, well, like a movie star to me. Much like a movie star though, she wasn't actually around much. The upside of that was I had a lot of freedom to play wherever I wanted, for as long as I wanted.

I usually went to my best friend Kara's house. Kara Crosby.

Kara lived five blocks away and her house was my favorite place to play. It was worth the walk. Kara's house was big and had lots of toys. Plus, Kara had this allure of cool and no stress. She never had trouble deciding what we should do or telling me what toys I could play with. And there was always something to eat.

Kara had two brothers: Marcello and Neil. Marcello was the oldest, then Neil, then Kara. Even though Neil was older than us, he'd been held back a year so he was in our grade, which basically made him our age. All three of the Crosbys were bigger than me, but they didn't hold back at all when we played. I was small, but strong, and sometimes a real contender in our games. I didn't usually try all that hard to compete with Kara. I didn't really want to win against her. But I sure did want to win against the boys. Especially Neil. The Crosbys always played hard, and if you won, you'd really done something.

When Kara's brothers got home from football practice we'd often play hide-and-go-seek. We'd tear around the house, our shrieks bouncing down the split staircase. Then sudden silence. Then, "Ready or not, here I come!" Our pleasure at the prospect of being caught squealed through the combined kitchen/family room letting everyone know when the person who was "it" was coming. As the sound reached a feverish pitch, we couldn't wait to be found. Instead, we jumped out of corners and cabinets and yelled "Boo!" then raced for base. I hear other people play it differently. They try sneaking back to base unnoticed. We'd never played that way though. The fun was in scaring the person who was "it."

We rarely played anything at my house. When it was just my mom and I at home, I usually stayed in my room with my paints, or my drawing notebook, or I read. If I wanted to play, I adventured out. But one time when I was about nine, my mom woke up in a good mood.

"Seffra, why don't you and your lil friends play over here for a change?" She even offered to pick up McDonald's.

"Really mom? Really?" I stepped from foot to foot like I was on hot coals. I was giddy. I couldn't wait to show off my cool mom to all my friends. I eagerly called Kara first, excited about the great time in store for us. Kara and her brothers came right over, along with a couple of other neighborhood kids Kara rounded up along the way. She was always the center of things like that. She knew what was going on and where to have the most fun and she let you come along if you were nice to her and did what she said, and everyone did, because she really did know where the best time was. And that day, the best time was going to be at my house.

My mom suggested hide-and-seek and we immediately agreed. I stood as upright as possible behind the pantry door. Goosebumps prickled my arms and I held my breath, suddenly needing to pee from the excitement of pursuit. My mom's heels clicked on the tile as she came around the corner toward me.

"Boo!" I yelled and jumped out.

The back of her arm struck my abdomen and the wind flew out of me as I hit the lemony linoleum floor. Pee soaked my underwear and I was horrified to find I'd wet my pants. I lay there, unsure what to do. Even more horrifying was the idea that one of the other kids might find out that I'd peed my pants. I lay still for what seemed an eternity before the idea struck: even through the pain, I was still hungry. The discomfort in my stomach redoubled as I realized there would be no McDonald's and my mom's mood was over. Kara stepped into the door frame but didn't say a word. My heart caught in my throat as I worried that Kara would humiliate me. She could call her brothers and all the other kids in and point and laugh and magnify my humiliation. Her eye met mine and she set her jaw and nodded.

"C'mon ya'll. We gotta get home. Neil, Marcello, everybody, let's go."

Kara'd saved me. She got everyone to leave without noticing what I'd done. She was my friend. I cried quietly as my friends listened to Kara and slinked home. My pee was the least of my concerns. Kara had at least taken care of that. But she couldn't do anything about my mom.

My mom spent the next few days in a mean, drugged stupor, slurring orders at me from the couch whenever I peeked out. "Get my cigarettes, you sneaky twat."

She was half-asleep with a cigarette between her fingers, but I didn't dare point that out. I said, "Yes, ma'am," and pretended to look for the mysterious, missing-cigarettes. Later, when she passed out, I slipped the still-lit cigarette from between her fingers and put it out in the brown ashtray on the end table, the ashtray that had almost certainly been lifted from a fast food restaurant.

I heard my mom get up in the night and stumble down the hall, ping-ponging off the walls. I heard dishes crash in the sink and her say, "Seffra, make the goddamned lan'lord fix the height of this toilet! I told you to call him."

She was peeing in the sink.

I stayed in my room hoping for my mom's mood to break, only venturing out to go to the bathroom, until the late afternoon sun slid away and hunger overtook me and I had to raid the kitchen for food. I tread as lightly as I could, but the floor squeaked and she snapped to attention. "You like hiding out in a kitchen so much, go on an' clean up those dishes while you're in there." She swirled her drink, motioning toward the sink of broken, pee-covered dishes from the night before, a mutter of *worthless brat* under her breath.

I stood, stuck to the yellow floor by grime and guilt and fear, unsure what to do.

"G'on! Clean it up. What are ya, simple?"

I worked carefully. I knew if I could do a good job and not upset her, my mom would feel better. She'd sober up and be nice again. We'd eat together and laugh.

I set to work, the shards of plain white dishes clinking quietly as my shaking hands placed them gently in the brown paper grocery bag we used for trash. I sniffed at the dishrag and, finding it didn't smell like pee, washed the unbroken dishes and wiped the white Formica table down. I used furniture polish because we didn't have any dish detergent. I must not have diluted the cleaner enough though because the whole room reeked of fake lemon when I was done, but at this point none of it curbed my hunger.

I set a pot on the stove placed some old Chinese take-out in it and tried not to think how long it had been in the fridge.

Crunchy rice pushed between my teeth as I chewed. I looked at a roach leg sticking out of the top of the wall near the ceiling where I'd thrown a shoe and killed it weeks before. I thought of the shooting. I pretended the bug was the bullet my father shot my mom with, lodged in the wall still. If I squinted slightly, I could only see a smudge and a black line like a crack. In my vision, the smudge was the bullet and the leg the cracked plaster.

And I was ashamed. Because I was envious of that imaginary bullet. I bounced from here to there and back again with my mom and her moods and her sudden trips and moves across the south and across the city. But the bullet had stayed. It forced a spot; cracked walls open to find its home and stayed right where it was. I imagined it was still in the wall of what might have been my childhood home. There it made a place for itself. It belonged.

I did not. I never belonged, even from birth. It was like that bullet took the place I should have had. I would spend a lot of my life trying to fight for the space that bullet took.

My mom was passed out again on the couch. And I hated her just then. I hated her for the rice between my teeth that took days to come loose. I hated her for making me pee my pants in front of all my friends. I hated her for drinking and smoking in our apartment and for making me wash dishes with furniture polish. I wished I hadn't put that cigarette out. I wished it had burned her fingers or worse, our whole dirty, cockroach-infested apartment. I took one of the knives I'd just washed out of the dish drainer and crawled under the table.

I leaned back and looked up at the underbelly of our kitchen table. Underneath you could see the pressed-together woodchips that were held by glue. The table was a farce. It wasn't wood and it wasn't Formica; it was slapped-together particleboard with something smoother on top.

I held the knife with both hands and pressed the tip in. The initial layer was waxy and gave way easily. I pressed harder and found a denser material with layers like tough ribbons you could cut through if you put enough force in. I pushed and dragged the knife through, enjoying the way the layers snapped like teeth breaking. I set my jaw and drew another line, and another and another. It satisfied something primal in me, and I zoned out while I worked. After a few more lines, I seemed to come to and leaned over to look. I'd made a jagged asterisk. The reality of what I'd done hit and I worried that my mom would find out. What would she do to me then?

I could imagine her, slapping me and screaming, "What, do you think ya' some kinda artist? This is what I get for givin' you nice art supplies" "Girl, you leave" slap, "my," slap, "things," slap, "*alone,*" She'd be screaming by the end. Or worse...

I shook it away. I hoped that she wouldn't notice. Maybe she'd never have reason to see underneath the table. Or maybe she wouldn't even think I'd done it if she did see. I tried to comfort myself with these possibilities, but I was a bad liar and a bad person. I knew she'd see it on my face and know I'd done it if she ever found those cuts. Why couldn't I just have stayed in my room and drawn in my notebook?

And I knew I was a shitty, stupid, evil twat. I put my face in my hands and rested like that before giving up and going back to my room and my mattress on the floor.

Uncle Phin, help. I fell asleep worrying. She'd been at it for days now, and I was really beginning to wonder when this binge might end. I fell asleep with the thin sheet over my head and old food churning in my stomach.

Then, the next day, as quickly as it started, it was over.

My mom sat at the kitchen table, freshly showered and dressed, smoking and reading August's Cosmo. It was 1991 and Paula Abdul was on the cover looking sexy in a swimsuit. I greedily took the scene in and wished for a hug. There was a plate with honey toast and a cup of tea. I ravaged the toast before leaving for school with a smack of my mom's lip-gloss on my forehead. She never found the asterisk. She was my real mom. Uncle Phin had listened and sent her back to take care of me.

2

I grew up in a shotgun apartment in downtown St. Louis. Well, really I grew up in several apartments in St. Louis, but I mostly remember the last one. I was born in rural Georgia, but because Social Services came knocking after the shooting, my mom put a comfortable six hundred miles between us and them. She kept us together. As soon as she got out of the hospital, she packed a bag and took a bus north. She picked St. Louis because she liked the idea of being on the Mississippi with the riverboats and the arch, plus she was almost out of money and the depot was there.

Our apartment had two small bedrooms and enough cockroaches to fill a few more. We lived three blocks from Kingshighway on the south side of the city.

South St. Louis is filled with brick buildings constructed around the turn of the century. The buildings are regular and boxy, yet lacking the distinguished smooth lines of Frank Lloyd Wright buildings in Chicago. Their foundations have settled, making for warped floors and tilting hallways, large rooms with high ceilings, which feel slightly off because of uneven floors. Sometimes you can still see where they used to load the ice for the old iceboxes. The radiators are loud clunking things that suck all the moisture out of the air and replace it with bangs, clanks, squeaks, and other abrupt noises that seem to occur almost entirely in the wee hours of the morning.

Tower Grove Park, a three-hundred-acre park conceived in 1868, was only a block away. It was filled with huge, green, grassy spots perfect for playing football or baseball or a giant game of tag. The park also boasted old white concrete pillars and steps leading to manmade ponds. The buildings were so old that green vines flourished in their cracks. At night, the neighbor kids and I used to dare each other to go further and further into the park, where streetlights couldn't expose the ancient ghosts we feared. I loved that park. I even loved the rush of excitement and fear I felt about those ghosts.

During the day, Tower Grove was where we went when we skipped school, a habit the whole neighborhood seemed to share. I'm not really sure who was left in my classroom some days, but someone must've been there because there were always worksheets waiting for me when I got back. Worksheets I'd just as soon as wiped my ass with, as do.

While we lived in St. Louis, my mom "worked" in Chicago. She made frequent trips there and sometimes I went; other times I didn't. The times I didn't get to go, I ached. Not going either meant being left behind at our apartment with a note and a mostly empty fridge, or it meant being dropped off at someone's house for a couple of days and it was anyone's guess whose house my mom'd pick.

When I did get to go to Chicago, I was guaranteed some time with my mom. The trips were a mixed bag but I always wanted to go because there would be fast food and a trip to the zoo or a park or somewhere exciting for me, and nothing compared to those outings my mom took me on when we went on our trips. There was a chance I wouldn't have a place to sleep but it was a chance I was fully willing to take. The chance of having to sleep on a dirty hotel room floor was totally worth my mom's attention and some good food. Besides, sometimes I did have a place to sleep, and sometimes that place was even in the same bed with my mom, with her wrapping her arms around me.

Trips to Chicago involved driving somewhere to pick up a vehicle that we'd then drive to Chicago. We'd stay a couple of days, often in more than one place, and then come home. As soon as we got back, we'd go to the Crosby's to drop off some money, switch cars, and hang out. Then we went home where my mom would usually sleep for a day or so.

In the spring of 1991 I was about to turn twelve. We were delivering a dusty, torn armchair and matching sofa bed. We'd ventured to a strange neighborhood I'd never seen on the north side of the city to leave our car and get the pickup with the furniture already loaded up.

"Remember Seffra, if we get pulled over, you don't say a word to the law." I was already looking down and nodding slowly. "Y'hear?"

She always said this bit about not saying a word to the law. It was very important to her. But all I cared about was the adventure and what new thing we were going to see. That and the food. I hadn't eaten in a while when we were leaving, but I wasn't about to complain. Food and fun came to me if I was patient on a trip to Chicago, but not if I complained.

By eight o'clock we were speeding down the highway with the windows open and the radio blasting. My mom looked beautiful with her wild hair whipping in the wind and her full lips stretched as she held the notes, singing along at the top of her lungs.

"They call me the voodoo woman/and I know the reason why," she cocked her head and squinted her eyes, putting all her soul into that song, just like a real jazz singer.

By nine o'clock my mom told me to go to sleep, but I didn't right away. While I knew to be patient, my growling stomach and the hope of food and adventure kept me up for a while. I turned the crank on the window, rolling it up and leaning my head against it. I closed my eyes and pretended to sleep but my growling stomach kept after me. After another hour, I mustered the courage to ask.

"Mama, I'm hungry. Are we still going to McDonald's?"

"It'll be half hour before we pass another one and it'll be closed by then. Go on to sleep now."

It was too late; McDonald's closed at ten on weekdays.

The sun was up now and I sat up, my cheek sticky with drool and tweed. I must've fallen asleep during the drive and been carried in when we'd arrived. I'd slept through the whole thing, though.

Now I was in a strange house sleeping on the couch we'd moved in the back of the pickup. The cushion underneath my head was recently cut open to retrieve the coke we'd really been delivering. I'd have thought they were idiots for not simply unzipping the cover except the hole made the perfect indent for my head. I put my hand between the rip and my face and felt the couch pattern pressed into my cheek from the material.

I got up and found the kitchen, where there was a note from my mom saying they'd gone out but would be back later and to make myself comfortable. There was no telling exactly when she'd be back. Sometimes it was an hour, sometimes not until the next day. But unlike at home when she disappeared, when we went to Chicago, I knew she'd be back within a day or so because she had work to do and a schedule to keep. And when someone was expecting you to come with money, you showed up where you were supposed to, when you were supposed to.

I checked the rest of the house and found no one home so I settled in. The house had olive green shag carpeting and dark wood paneling throughout, even in the kitchen. The décor made it dark, even in the daylight, so I turned as many lights on as I could and opened my notebook and drew for a while but nothing really panned out.

I set my pencils down, stretched and looked around. This was going to be good. We had a house with three bedrooms to stay at (instead of a rent-by-the-hour or by-the-week hotel room) with food *and* cable. I fixed myself a glass of water in a drive-thru promotional glass with princess Leia on the side and found some chips and settled on the couch to watch MTV. I danced around to the Top 20 Countdown, vogueing along with Madonna and jumping from the couch to the floor and back again, as though it were the stairs Paula Abdul danced up in the video to "Opposites Attract." I twisted and turned while jumping and singing along at the top of my lungs to all the songs they played. Finally, out of breath, I clicked the TV off and headed for the shower.

I stepped out of my clothes leaving them in a scrunched up pile on a towel (the cleanest thing I could think to do.) I pulled shower shoes out of my overnight bag, a must-have on these trips because the olive green tub had white scum in polluted waves around the rim and black grime was all over the tile. But a gross shower was nothing to worry about with shower shoes and top 40 in my head, so I kept enjoying my own private dance party.

I snacked all day, eating cans of ravioli and making myself Tapioca on the stove. That evening I watched a movie, sprinting to the bathroom during commercials because I'd pilfered and drank an entire 2-liter-bottle of soda. When the caffeine finally wore off, I fell asleep on the couch close to midnight.

I jerked awake to my mother and her friends coming home. I checked the clock on the VCR. 3:09 a.m. The bars must've closed. I rubbed my eyes and tried to blend into the couch, hoping to get an idea of what kinds of friends these were. Nice and funny, or mean and drugged? You had to approach them differently. If they were drunk and dumb, it was best to hole up somewhere like a closet or bathroom until they all passed out. But if they were funny, I liked staying up late for the after-party with my mom.

There was a guy with a leather jacket and thick brown beard; a woman with a Harley t-shirt frayed at the bottom; and several other non-descript biker-types. Then there was my mom, with full make-up and a slow smile. It was almost springtime and the weather was changing. The nights were still cold but with that dewy promise of something nice. The crickets were just waking up.

This seemed like a group who could probably be navigated pretty easily. They'd be the type who listened if I said something, but ignored me if I didn't. I could stay up or go to bed. Either would be fine and there looked to be no need to hide from anyone scary, which was good. I was thinking of going to bed when a guy with pale blue eyes the color of expensive pool table felt strolled in. He was older than me for sure, but only maybe nineteen, and he was gorgeous. He pushed his long brown hair back over his shoulder and stood tall. I swooned.

"This is my daughter, Seffra, ya'll." I glowed for a moment before pushing the feeling down. *Be cool.*

"Hi." I waved my hand close to my face, then jerked it back into my lap.

His smile made him even more gorgeous. His straight, white teeth were framed by full lips and his eyes were clearly in on the fun. This was going to be good.

I excused myself and went to the bathroom where I pulled out my makeup bag and hurriedly applied eye shadow and bright lipstick in an attempt to look older. I left my satin button-down pajamas on since I was pretending to have woken up this way and didn't want him to think I was getting dressed up for him. I jumped up and down a few times, talked to myself in the mirror pretending to be talking to him, then kissed myself in the mirror.

"Ew, puh. Gross!" I spit everything I could into the toilet, then wiped my tongue with a square of toilet paper. I hacked a few more times, spitting the bits of tissue paper out.

A knock came, followed by a deep voice asking, "You alright in there?"

Oh god, please don't let it be him. I thought. Then rushed out, looking down.

"I'm fine." Black boots. Whew, thankfully it was the biker guy.

I went out to the kitchen where the girl in the Harley t-shirt was wiping her nose and sniffing and saying, "Aw shit." The men were standing around talking and laughing holding brown beer bottles. Without saying anything, I slid up and sat on the counter and listened in. They were arguing about music and I waited until I was pretty sure the gorgeous guy was listening and then casually asked, "Ever heard of 2 Live Crew?"

He was a metal guy and didn't like rap. I stuck to my plan to try and prove how cool and grown up I was by explaining that "a bunch of the guys went to jail for rapping such dirty stuff." Then added, "It's fucked up."

My mom had her arm around the woman in the belly shirt and they both laughed and stumbled. They were lost in their own conversation that had likely been repeated many times by now and become both louder and more hilarious as the night wore on.

"Yeah, I don't like rap, but that *is* fucked up," he said and I wanted to think of anything to say that would keep his eyes on me. I was about to make something up about meeting them in concert when the slutty girl came over. She and my mom were finished with whatever inside joke and the girl started frenching him just like that. She took his hand and led him down the hall and through a door, calling out "G'night," before locking it closed.

I went back to sitting on the counter and stayed up telling the same four jokes over and over to the biker guy because I couldn't understand anything he was saying anyway but he laughed every time. Then he threw up next to the couch.

"Damnit! That's where my daughter's supposed t' sleep, damn fool."

Dawn was sneaking in to the dark house, and my mom took my hand and led me to a bedroom with a queen-sized mattress and box spring on the floor and I gratefully crawled in with her. She kicked me a few times then snuggled me and kissed my arm.

"I love you," she mumbled, before slumping over, her slobber glomming onto my forearm.

"What Mom?" I whispered. I sat up and shook her gently. "Mom?" But she was asleep.

The next day around noon, she took me to McDonald's before taking me on our outing. I wolfed down my entire meal and was finishing the end of my strawberry milkshake when I realized I would still be hungry and should've taken more time savoring it all. I looked up at my mom. She'd barely touched her food.

"You can have the rest. I'm not hungry." She pushed the tray toward me.

"Aren't you gonna eat any of it?"

"Naw, baby. I'm just not hungry." She drew out the word in her southern drawl. *Huhn-gry.* I eagerly ate almost all of her food too, leaving only the blackest bits of burnt fries and an edge of tartar sauce-covered bun.

As I finally slowed to a ballooned-up halt with my eating, my mom got an excited look.

"Guess where I'm takin' you this trip."

"A park?"

"Better."

"Shopping?".

"Better."

"Are you going to tell me?"

"It's a surprise."

We got up to go.

It was warm and we drove with the windows down. I wanted to be outside. After swearing through traffic and parallel parking for what felt like hours, we approached a dark grey, imposing rectangular building with its simple lines

"The Chicago Museum of Modern Art," she announced to me.

I thought, *This is it? Who cares?*

I hoped it wouldn't take long and that I could politely make my way through quickly so that we could head out to eat again sooner than later.

I tried my hardest to feign excitement.

The massive doors opened surprisingly easily and all of me quieted in the large echoing space of the museum. I stepped inside and took in all the work.

The concern I'd had moments before about impending boredom evaporated instantly. I wandered rooms filled with huge paintings covered in thick slurred colors that screamed feelings.

My mom walked with me through most of the museum for a while, but I stopped to stare and think longer than she did. Soon she was out of sight.

I spent what felt like a lifetime on this one piece, a sculpture where an entire room was given over to a 20' by 20' pane of glass suspended in tact over an untold amount of broken glass below. The whole display was roped off which was good because I wanted to step on all that glass. It was brutal.

I didn't want to leave.

Eventually I continued through the museum, drinking in all the emotion, utterly lost in it. There was a sculpture of a brass woman with drawers pulling out of her legs and a larger-than-life mobile in all black and white that hung over the stairs between floors. There was a painting that somehow seemed like stairs heading in every direction, changing "up" into "down" and making sideways into a question. The art was raw emotion and I was completely taken in.

I had no idea how long I'd been wandering, rapt in this new world. I came to a painting by Gustav Klimt of a bare-breasted woman who was pregnant. There were disks of color and all this red, and these three ladies with their heads turned and their eyes closed like they were listening to the floor. There was something calm on the pregnant woman's face and it seemed to come from the ladies below her in her dress. For some reason it reminded me of my mother. I wondered if she'd been supported by all kinds of people when she was pregnant the way the woman in the painting had been.

Suddenly, I got nervous about where my mom was. I hadn't seen her in a while. What if she left me? I felt an internal frenzy rising and rushed around looking for her. I found her smoking on a bench in the afternoon sun.

She smiled. "What did you think?"

I smiled and shook my head.

Her look was hard to read for a moment. "So, what? You didn't like it. I shoulda known you'd be ungrateful."

I shook my head wildly. "No, Mama. I loved it." I drew out the word loved and dropped my jaw.

She pulled her sunglasses down and glared at me.

"Really, Mama. It was amazing. It's my favorite place you've taken me."

"You know, you could say thank you ev'ry once in a while." She put her cigarette out and stood up and we left. "I ain't tryin' to raise no ungrateful jezebel. Yeah, don't think I didn't see that makeup you put on last night and that you never bothered to take off before bed."

I touched my face and looked down, bracing myself in case she kept on, in case she hit me or worse, humiliated me. "Thank you, ma'am."

She reached out her hand and cupped my face with it. I smelled the fresh cigarette smoke mixing with the new spring air and her perfume and it was all clean. She tilted my face up toward her and smiled. "I told you it was better than the zoo."

I smiled into the sun.

She slid her sunglasses up her nose. "Best we get goin' now."

It was a front. She wasn't going to slap me or anything. She was raising me right was all. She was just reminding me to be polite and a good girl. I was so happy and so lucky. I'd gotten to do something cool with her and I wanted more. The trees were budding and the world was alive with energy and possibility.

3

In my first memory, I'm a toddler wearing pink panties with ruffles on the butt. I'm only supposed to wear them under my Sunday dress but I'm wearing them now. I sit on shag carpet and pick around in its pile long enough to find a straight pin. I stare at the head of the pin and press its point against my fingertip. It hurts and I'm mad so I throw it on the floor.

I stop and inhale deeply through my nose. I hold the humidity in and the scent is filled with a thousand minerals as though the Midwest earth had been filtered through this carpet. It is fecund. Earlier I lay face down in this carpet and sniffed and sniffed at that smell until my cheek was scratchy and red. But this never brought me sleep and I was supposed to nap.

Napping is a far away possibility now. I couldn't possibly. Not with the plywood shelves filled with toys. I sit down on my blue plastic booster seat and survey the low shelves for what to play with. I settle on some primary-colored rubber blocks and get to it.

I've been playing for a long time. Long enough to hear the dehumidifier whirring and then clunking off, then shrugging into service again several times over. I feel the need to pee rising up. I pinch and squeeze. Squeeze harder. The feeling passes and I return to my game.

The booster seat gets sweaty and slippery and I wipe it off and sit back down. Even dry it's too warm, so I sit down on the carpet again.

I sit forward, trying to hold my urine. The long carpet strands of mustard yellow mix in with the off-white and dark greens and they are cool at first. Rough, but cool. I listen for adults and hear nothing but a clunking dryer.

A wave of the feeling comes again and I squeeze. Again, it passes and I can return to stacking blocks: red, blue, red, blue until I run out or the stack falls. I build a more stable, less color-coordinated stack and put other toys on top. The toys are talking to each other.

"Shhh she's sleeping. Let's dance," a blue square says to a green long piece.

I let them continue and don't tell them I'm awake. They throw themselves around in a frenzied dance party. Once the pieces are exhausted and lying scattered across the floor, the wave comes again and I cross my legs tighter, sit further forward. The need is coming more frequently now. The concentration and squeezing to stop it is harder each time. I should go upstairs and go potty, I think. But I never have this much fun playing. So I squeeze and squeeze and squirm to squeeze harder than I can.

Plus, I'm supposed to be napping. I squeeze and hold my breath to keep it in check. I keep playing. I can't reach all the blocks now while still squeezing and holding it, so I play only with the blocks that are next to me. I promise myself, in just a minute, I'll go. In one minute, I'll pretend to be sleeping and just waking up and go to the potty and it'll all be fine. A minute comes and goes and I play it away. More minutes.

I'm out of bargaining and *need* to go now. Finally, I try to stand up. I am as far from the bathroom as I could possibly be. I picture the path back up the stairs, past the kitchen table, straight down the nice-blue-carpeting to the bathroom door. It's too far. I have to stop and sit back down if I'm going to make it that far. I sit back down so I can rock and hold it in better. I rock and rock, and squeeze. I can't stand up now. I have to go too badly. I hope for a solution. I rock and hope. It comes eventually.

Even as I pee on the floor, shame and relief pooling in my pink ruffles, I think, "I should stop." I could pinch and stop it, then run up the stairs to the bathroom to finish. I think that would be better. My mom would be less disappointed if I couldn't hold it but tried. I think this as I let go, give in to the shame, give in to the spreading consequences, and empty the whole thing.

The relief is total at first and I feel so much better. I think about picking up the toys and resuming my game with them but there is pee all over the blocks I've been playing with and the farther away ones seem so far now. I know my mother will be angry with me because I know how to use the big girl potty and I shouldn't have accidents.

The solution, I think, is to lie on the floor, pretending to be asleep. This way, my mother will think I've slept through an accident. I might not get in trouble then.

I look at the door, wondering when she might come in, when relief from this soggy warm floor will come.

I lay my head into the carpet only to find the pee has soaked over this far and I get it on my face. I'm too scared to even cry though I really want to. I don't want anyone to hear me and come in. I sit back up and feel around on the floor for a better spot to put my head down.

The ruffles are scratchier now that they're wet but I don't want to itch them and get the nasty on my hands. My head is heavy and the carpet around me is getting colder. At first it feels good. I've been so hot. I look at the dark wooden door and think it's opening but it's not. I lay my head back down.

I doze a little and am on the edge of actual sleep when the cold of the soggy carpet starts to get to me. I shiver. It's as though my underpants are the scratchy side of a cold, wet, pee-soaked sponge. I shiver and look at the door. It's still not opening so I take my panties off hoping it will help.

It does help and I fall asleep finally. My mom comes in and picks me up and I think I'm saved for a moment. My eyes flutter open and I see the look on her face change from love to disgust.

"Seffra, baby, what did you..?" Realization, disgust. "You nasty, nasty thing!"

She drops me and starts smacking my naked bottom. The tears I held back come hard, harder than the slaps.

"You shut your nasty, nasty, diz-gustin' mouth!" she growls in my ear. But I don't stop crying or even slow down.

She picks up the cold, wet, pink ruffled underpants and holds them over my mouth and keeps smacking and smacking my naked bottom. I can taste the sweet acrid smell intertwining in my nose and mouth with the scratchy ruffles. I can still taste it even now. I hate pink ruffles.

The next memory I have of my mother, I'm about five years old and we're going to the library. It's a rainy spring day and I'm skipping alongside my mother on our way through Tower Grove Park holding my mom's hand. I'm wearing bright yellow galoshes and I kick at the water in a puddle when I think she won't notice. She smiles down at me and I really let 'er rip, kicking at the water for all I'm worth. I love going to the library and the added bonus of an umbrella and access to puddles is almost more than a kid could ask for.

"Okay, that's enough, Seff," she says sweetly, smiling down at me.

I hold my umbrella to the side so I can hold her smile in my heart. A few drops of rain fall on my head. The rain is letting up and the sun is shining through even as the last holdouts drop on us.

As we get close to the steps that lead up to the library's entrance, I hear a man's voice resonating and rhyming almost like in the Dr. Seuss books my mom never wants to read because they're too long.

He looms large. I look up and the rain stops completely. I lay my umbrella down on the wet sidewalk. He's standing on top of a milk crate, dancing and talking about God. He smiles at me and his eyes sparkle.

My mom takes my hand and pulls me behind her, shielding me from this man. "Pick up your umbrella and let's go."

My mom's dragging me and I'm tripping, walking sideways to see his sparkling eyes and the rainbow that's beginning in the background.

"Is that what God looks like?" I want to know.

"That's homeless trash. Now, c'mon." my mom tells me and drags me through the enormous wooden doors.

I try to look, but never get another chance. I don't want to anger her, especially because there's nothing I want as badly as I want to sit in my mother's lap while she reads a story that rhymes. Still, Boogie, the homeless man, his eyes and his rhymes stay with me and I hope I'll see him again.

4

On my twelfth birthday, my mom took me for a short trip to the mall. In 1991 the mall was the coolest place to be and I always felt extra cool strutting up to the doors with her. She was stylish and pretty and people usually thought she was my older sister. She wore a tight pleather jacket that hugged her tiny hourglass frame. Out of the bottom peeked a few inches of short blue jean skirt. Rain had just let up and her high heels click-clacked as she strode across the slick sidewalk. We headed into the mall through the large glass entrance nearest the food court and the arcade.

We skipped the food court and she marched me straight down the steps to the arcade where she fed bills into the machine in exchange for fistfuls of quarters.

"What're we doing?" I asked. I didn't really like video games that much and she knew that.

"You'll see," she said with a grin that implied she had something up her sleeve.

"But you said we only have a little while," I whined.

"Hush and come on now." She walked on purposefully while I followed behind. We went back upstairs and down the large walkway leading to the main shopping area. Along the way, I peered around, looking for clues as to what she might have in store.

In the center of one plaza area, she stopped at a bouncy ball vending machine and put in quarter after quarter.

"Grab 'em," she told me cranking the dial on the machine.

When my fists and hers were both so full we were dropping balls all over the place, she took off toward the exit, throwing fistfuls into the air behind her. I caught on and did the same, running full speed to catch up. Just before I got to the doors, I stopped and turned.

In that moment, there were balls suspended in the air of all sizes and colors. Pink, and blue, and yellow dots glowed in the light airy space at staggered heights of anywhere from 25 feet down to the ground. They were bouncing off of every smooth surface of the large, high-ceilinged walkway: stone walls, hard-tiled floor, glass storefronts, colors flitting everywhere. It was amazing.

I stepped outside after her, letting the doors shut behind me with all that magic still bouncing around like a racing heartbeat. I laughed aloud and chased her back to the car.

But that wasn't the end of our day together. From the mall, we went to the grocery store where my mom sprung for three different half-gallons of ice cream and a name brand frozen cheese pizza: my favorite.

When we got home, my mom played game after game of cards with me. We played Go Fish and War and 21. We laughed and laughed and then I ate until I almost puked.

When I yawned and said I was ready for bed, my mom smiled warmly. After I'd tucked myself under the covers, she appeared in my doorway.

"Birthday's not over yet," she said and handed me a small box.

I tore open the paper and lifted the lid. Inside there was a necklace with a pendant from the art museum we'd visited in Chicago. It was a broken piece of glass from the exhibit I'd seen and liked so much. The rough places on the shard had been smoothed out so it wouldn't cut you.

"I know our life is pretty rough sometimes," she said. "I love you though."

"Thank you," I whispered, barely able to get the words out.

"I know my girl," she told me and left the room.

I wore it from that day on.

My mom was the best. I never wanted the day to end. I could be with my mom forever, eating ice cream and having adventures.

But that wasn't going to be our life. I didn't have forever left with my mom. At least not living with her. I had less than a year. I didn't know that yet though. I had no idea as I pulled the covers up to my chin. The rain started back up just in time to block out all the noise in our lives and lull me to sleep. The sounds of fights and drunks were long gone. I had rain. The smells of urine and whiskey blocked out by pizza and ice cream. And in my mind's eye, I didn't see the bullet hole or the cracked plaster walls. I saw a future filled with bouncy balls and a beautiful necklace.

5

A requirement of graduation from 6th grade into junior high was that we complete 20 hours of volunteer work. I resented the requirement at first, but I'd always loved dogs and hated school. So that spring when my 6th grade teacher, Mr. Miller, reminded me that I had completed exactly none of the required hours and offered the suggestion that I do it at an animal shelter walking dogs, I jumped. He even offered me the chance to leave school a little early.

One afternoon, I was walking Sadie, my favorite. She was a giant Burmese Mountain Dog mix who was terrified of everything and loved only me. I wanted to celebrate getting to take Sadie out with a trip to Tower Grove Park or even Forest Park (which was a little closer) but I didn't have quite enough time.

Instead, I walked her all over the Hill, the neighborhood where the shelter was located. The Hill is an Italian neighborhood in South St. Louis filled with small, well-kept brick bungalows in neat rows where the lawns are well cared for and the neighbors drink lemonade by invitation in their back yards.

I had to tug Sadie along as she whined and whimpered about overturned tricycles and sudden noises. She spooked easy. I scratched behind her ear and sweet-talked and then tugged her to entice her onward. It wasn't like when we went to Tower Grove or Forest Park and she finally relaxed. Today, we had only time to take a walk on the Hill and that would have to be enough.

As we walked, I strutted my stuff down the block with the huge beast I was proud to have tamed. Then I forgot to be cool and pulled on the leash, playing with Sadie. She galumphed and stomped playfully with her front paws down and her tail wagging in the air practically above my head.

I made a *boof* noise at her and jumped back. "C'mon girl. Back to our walk."

We fell into a rhythm and I was soon off in my own world. I didn't have to tug anymore and only rarely had to guide her around any terrifying booby traps like an opening garage door. We walked and our feet kept time.

My reverie was interrupted though when I heard a voice somewhere. "Mmm pussy..." it whispered and echoed. There was something familiar about the voice, but also dreamlike. It was definitely loud enough that I was sure I'd heard it, but it sounded both loud and far away.

"What the hell?" I looked around, but I didn't see a soul anywhere.

"Mmm take that skirt off, little girl." I heard it again.

Sadie put her ears back and hung her head. I frantically scanned the horizon but still did not see a single person anywhere. She began tugging on the leash to get me to head the other way but I was curious. I tied her to a tree and resumed looking for the boy.

"Hey, over here." I heard a boy's laugh echo.

"Who is that?" I demanded.

I listened, hard. "Seriously, who's there?"

More laughing, and yes, a definite echo. I was so frustrated at not being able to locate the noise that I'd forgotten to think about what the boy had said.

"You wanna fuck me?" the boy asked.

Excitement and revulsion both shot through me like an impulse. I kept looking. I got closer to the sound, but somehow I still wasn't seeing where the person was.

"What the hell?"

A mixture of taunting laughter and downright giggles.

"You're getting closer."

I cautiously stepped forward.

"Closer."

I took another step.

"Nice panties."

"You can't see my underwear, liar." I knew whoever it was he must be full of shit.

"Yes I can. They're blue and they have little white stars on them."

I had absolutely no idea whether he was right or not. I hopped up on the curb, walked over to the tree where Sadie was tied up and crouched behind her to check. Sadie whined but I ignored her and looked at my underwear.

He was right. How the hell did he see them?

I walked back. "Okay, where are you?"

"Warmer…"

I stepped up on the curb.

"Warmer…"

I took another step onto the grass.

"Colder."

Huh? How could I have gotten colder? Where the hell was this guy? I looked around. There were no trees to hide up in except the one Sadie was tied to and besides he'd told me I was colder when I got closer to the tree. It wasn't possible. There was literally nowhere he could be.

"Alright, fuck it. If you aren't going to tell me where you're at, I'm outa here."

"Down here, stupid."

"Down where?" I said stepping back and squatting, holding my skirt carefully. I tilted my head and peered into the sewer. Neil was there. He'd crawled into the street drainage where our baseballs and ping pong balls always ended up. That was why I couldn't find him with the hotter/colder game. I was standing on top of where he was.

"How'd you get down there?" I asked.

"How do you think I got down here?"

"I don't know, hemorrhoid-breath, that's why I'm asking!"

"I lifted up the manhole cover, duh."

"Huh? How?" I continued, skeptical. "It's too heavy. You couldn't have lifted that."

"Sure I coulda."

"Nu uh. No way. Those things weigh like 500 pounds."

"I'm really strong."

"I've beat you at pull ups. I'm stronger than you and there's *no* way I could lift one of those things. Not unless, like, a building were on fire and I had a crap-ton of adrenaline."

"You are *not* stronger."

"Am too."

We argued back and forth until I admitted that he *might* be as strong as me. I was always competing with Neil. He was the only kid in my grade that could beat me in a race. I was faster at distance, but he could bob and weave and get past me in a game of tag. I could do all my times tables correctly, but he could read harder books. I could do more pull-ups than him (I was smaller) but he could beat me at arm wrestling.

"The cover was off already," he admitted then.

I noticed the metal lid tipped up and slid to the side where he must've squirmed past and gone down. He was the skinniest of the Crosbys.

"What's it like down there?"

"Why don't you come down here and find out?"

"No way, grosso. I heard the creepy things you said to me a few minutes ago."

"Have it your way."

I regretted saying no and wanted to go down there. I wanted to keep it going. I peered around, trying to find him. "C'mon seriously, what's it like down there? You sound like you're pretty far down there and I can't really see you."

Suddenly I saw his face in the space between the street and the sidewalk where the water drained during heavy rains.

"Ah!" I said jumping back, laughing.

"It's cool. There's a ladder that goes to the bottom—"

"Bow-wowowWOW." Sadie'd had enough. Her whine had turned to loud barking.

A guy with a thick Italian accent opened the red painted door of the house we were in front of and said, "What's goin' on out here?"

I heard the street light buzz and looked up to see it flickering on. Shit, I was late.

"I gotta go," I said to Neil. I dusted my knees off and grabbed Sadie, untying her leash and we ran all the way home. I popped in, still panting, and told my mom I would run Sadie back to the shelter and be right back. When I got back, my mom was gone. She left a note.

"Sort the dirty laundry and don't make any messes. I'll be back later."

I had all night to think about the things Neil had said.

All of them.

6

One night shortly after the incident with Neil, I awoke to the crash of glass breaking. I sat up and sorted out that the sound must've been someone dropping a drink and the glass breaking on the floor. I heard my mom and her friends laughing. I pulled my pillow up over my head and hummed to block out the noise. I had school the next day and I didn't feel like hanging out for a party. I was too tired. Plus I didn't want to miss school now that I got to walk the dogs afterwards. The pillow worked and I drifted back to sleep.

What felt like a moment later, I woke to a chill up my spine and opened my eyes to see a man standing in my doorway. I held the piece of glass, the pendant from my necklace in my fingers. The man was silhouetted by the harsh hallway light, which was white and unforgiving behind him. It blinded me and I remember hearing him panting and wondering for a moment if something was wrong with him. Maybe he was having a heart attack. But I felt prickly in my stomach and the chill hadn't left my spine so I kept breathing as silently as I could, waiting.

I remembered a nightmare in my bones and wondered if I was awake. It was this recurring nightmare where someone was robbing us and if I stayed perfectly still and didn't breathe, the robber would leave us alone. But if I made even the slightest movement, he'd kill us. So, in my dream I'd lay as still as possible. It was like I'd already practiced this in my sleep. So I knew just what to do.

I stayed perfectly still. *Huff, huff.* My eyes were so wide I wondered if he would catch a glint of them like a cat's in the night, but I didn't dare blink. A deep growl and then more huffing and puffing. I was definitely awake and this was real. The piece of glass on the pendant of my necklace was pressed so hard against the palm of my hand, it was starting to hurt. I didn't dare loose my hold or move at all, not even micro movements.

Then, I heard my mom's heels stumble down the hallway and her say, "What the...? Get your God-damn despicable ass out ah MY HOUSE." She was screaming by the end and threw her shoe at him. I heard his belt buckle clatter as he turned and ran. He ran, holding his pants, and she chased him screaming all the way. "Get OUT." Then, everyone was quiet for a moment.

I sat up and waited, still not daring to blink. My eyes were now fully adjusted to the bright light from the hallway. I heard whispers and the front door to our apartment opening and closing as everyone left the party. I let the pendant go and rubbed my hand.

My mom came back and her warm, whiskey-breath covered my face. She asked over and over "Are you alright, baby?" and "He didn't hurt ya, did he?" Followed by, "If he touched one hair on my baby's head, I swear. TO. GOD..." through clenched teeth.

She was too drunk to realize how many times she'd already asked so she kept me up the rest of the night. She asked over and over again. She'd seem to wear out and tell me that if anything like that ever happened again, I was to tell her immediately and "I swear-ah, Ah'll kill 'em." Swear always had two syllables when my mother said it but she put even more emphasis on the word. And I'd hope we were done and I could go to bed but then she'd start up again. "Did that man touch you, baby?" I'd shake my head no, and she'd swear she'd kill any man who touched me. "I protect my baby." Finally she started to drift off.

Suddenly she sat up and said clearly, "No man will treat my baby like some common jezebel." Then slurring again, "Men are filthy pigs and if you let'm, they'll make you filthy too." And she fell asleep.

It felt good, being protected by my mom. But now I couldn't sleep. So I tried reading to calm down. I liked to read. It passed the time and gave me something else to think about when my mom was gone or when there was a party in the house that I didn't want in on. It was another land to be in. Another set of problems for someone else to solve.

I read *War of the Worlds,* trying to figure out what the aliens looked like with their slender limbs. But after reading the same passage several times without comprehending anything, I gave up in favor of thinking about infinity and the ceiling.

I pushed on my eyelids with the tips of my fingers. Harder, and harder until the little fireworks happened that I loved. The light bursting colorful and white against the velvety blackness made me think about infinity and where that might be. What it might mean— forever and ever and ever and ever. Nothingness.

But my mind wandered back to the warmth and wonder of my mom's movie-star attention, her protection. It was all I wanted. All I could want. And right now I had it. I'd earned it. I'd been good and still and now she'd take care of me. Forever and ever and nothingness and eternity.

"Uncle Phin, if you're listening, keep me with my mom. Please. Forever and ever, amen."

Then, abruptly, my mind stalled on Neil in the manhole and there was a small hard pit in my stomach. Out shot a sprout. A green length of guilt that lets you know something is your fault; you've done something wrong. I swore I smelled urine and thought of the panties I'd worn when I wet my pants when I was little. I thought of the underwear I'd had on that Neil had seen. They were balled up in the corner of my closet. I couldn't bring myself to wash them.

I remembered the things Neil whispered and how even though I knew it was sleazy, knew it was wrong, I liked the attention. I knew that somehow I had caused what happened with that silhouetted man. I didn't deserve my mother's protection or her love. That sprout was splitting the distance between my mom and me.

I liked hearing Neil's dirty words, feeling that filthy male attention. And I knew—there was something wrong with me, something without a name. Something that made me look dirty and available to men. I curled up, crying as silently as I could and holding my stomach, willing the pit to grow smaller and darker. But it didn't disappear. Instead it had a slender green sprout anchoring it. That sprout, that guilt, wasn't going anywhere.

I asked Uncle Phin for help. "Uncle Phin?" I prayed. "Please make me good. If you could just help get rid of this rock in my stomach, then maybe I could stop being so gross and evil. So, you know, help me if you can. Please? Thanks."

And even though I knew I didn't deserve it, I snuggled into my mom and inhaled deeply. I smelled vanilla and cigarettes and dryer sheets before drifting off. I reveled in her protection.

The next day I lied to myself about it all. I glared at Neil, rolled my eyes at him and mouthed "you're nasty." I hoped the lie would be enough to keep me close to my mom. I held my necklace tight. I hoped it would be enough to grant me her protection. I wanted the lie.

But after school on my way to Kara's, I paid attention to that sewer cover. It was a slightly rusted metal against newly poured concrete. The street was smooth and swept free of debris. But down below, where I looked, it echoed of murk and wetness and I got a little jolt up my spine as I secretly hoped Neil would be in there.

7

I went to Kara's after school lots of times. Lately though, we hadn't been doing as much hide-and-seek playing. We were about to be teenagers, or at least, she was. I had almost a year left of being twelve. I wanted to be decisive and grown up like teenagers and Kara and my mom. So we'd given up street ball and kick-the-can in favor of doing each other's hair and makeup while watching MTV. Sometimes we'd prank call boys we liked.

"What would you do if Neil tried to kiss you?" Kara asked when I told her about the manhole cover.

"Ew. I told you what he said. Why would I kiss him?"

"Because, dummy, you could learn on him so you'd know what to do when a really hot guy wants it."

I felt a jolt thinking of him wanting *it*.

"You wanna help me practice for when Sidney tries to kiss me?" Kara liked a boy at the middle school named Sidney. I scrunched my eyebrows and turned my head slightly. Kara looked me right in the eye. She wasn't kidding.

"What? I'm not gay. I don't want him to think I don't know what I'm doing. He's older and sexy and black and I want him to know that I'm woman enough to handle all that." She exhaled dramatically. "Just help me out a little. I need practice." She was almost whining. "Or do you like my *brother*?"

"I do not. You know I don't like anyone right now."

She rolled her eyes, challenging me on this point. I pushed back. "Your dad would kill you if he knew you liked a black guy, you know,"

She shrugged. "He's too into your mom to notice right now anyway."

My eyes grew wide.

"What? You've got to be kidding me. How could you not know? I mean, she's over here, like, all the time and they're always taking off for Chicago together."

"That's work," I answered aloud but thought, *So that's why she hadn't been taking me with her lately.*

"Oh yeah, *work.* Obviously." She rolled her eyes. I was so naïve. "I've heard them fucking. She's nasty, dude. He can't say shit to me about Sidney."

One time when Kara and I were about six, we touched tongues just to see. We'd seen my mom kissing her boyfriend and their tongues pink and fat coming out the corners of their mouths. It was awful. It felt rough and slimy at the same time. After that, I'd sometimes fold my own tongue on top of itself imagining grownups kissing. I couldn't for the life of me imagine anyone wanting to do that on purpose.

"So how 'bout it? Help me out here."

I snapped to. "I guess," I said and she pulled a wad of gum out of her mouth and started kissing me, still holding it in her fingers.

But kissing Kara didn't feel like sand paper and slime. And so we kept doing it. Every time I came over we did it. At first we only kissed. But then we started turning it into a pretending game where we took all our clothes off. She told me to pretend I was the girl and she was the boy so I could learn what I was supposed to do. She'd touch my chest and pretend I had breasts. She'd also touch between my legs and that was the part I liked. She rubbed between my legs and

I thought of Neil and the manhole cover. And I wanted her to keep rubbing and rubbing.

We'd been doing this pretty regularly for a while and had gotten a little careless about where we were. We usually played in her room, but this time we were in the living room. Her living room had a new sofa and matching loveseat. They were overstuffed light brown corduroy. They sat in an *L* with a black leather La-Z-Boy rounding out the arc that faced the black, lacquered entertainment center where the TV and stereo were. The love seat was just the right size to fit us both and it made me feel protected to be with her in the tight space with our backs to the hallway. We could duck into it and no one could see us.

We were usually careful about listening for her brothers and her dad and would race to put our clothes back on and pretend to be arm wrestling when anyone came. But that was with the protection of a bedroom that has a door. We'd grown overconfident. This time, with no door, careless in the living room, completely naked and caught up in mentally begging her to keep going, I didn't hear her dad come in.

"What do you two think you're doing?" he demanded.

We were paralyzed with fear. The rain on the windows seemed to still, not dripping while we waited for our sentencing.

"Kara, go to your room and think about what you've done."

Fear wrapped in shame stalked all corners. She didn't even bother to grab her clothes, she just ran for it.

I couldn't stop thinking of my clothes on the floor. I was freezing now and felt more naked than I'd ever been in my entire life. Unconsciously I reached my hand up for my necklace, but I'd taken it off and it was in the pile with my clothes. I stood, my eyes burning from not blinking.

Finally I asked, "Uh, are you gonna tell my mom?" I was too sick to my stomach to even think about crying.

"I might." He spoke slowly. "I might not." He rubbed his thumb and index finger together, turning over how he could use this new information, what he could get out of it. Suddenly he snapped out of it and seemed to remember me. And I realized he wasn't going to tell. He looked right at me and I knew I wasn't going to *my* room.

"Seffra, you know what you were doing with my daughter?"

I didn't answer.

He looked at me—steady, cruel. "That's what I thought."

I kept standing there, growing colder by the moment. Goosebumps covered my arms but I fought not to shiver. I glanced at my clothing, in a pile on the carpet in the middle of the room, Mr. Crosby looming in the doorway.

He stepped the rest of the way into the room and sat down in the La-Z-Boy. The leather squeaked. A shiver escaped and I was suddenly shaking.

"Oh, you'll be okay. Don't worry, now." I heard his belt buckle and the leather gave a shrill adjustment to his weight-shift. "Bend over and touch your toes."

He panted for a moment and I stopped shaking. I floated above myself and the sounds stopped. He didn't touch me and I didn't feel or think. I wasn't cold. I wasn't anything.

"I won't tell your mother about this for now. But you make sure you remember who your friends are." He pinched my naked bottom then and I jolted upright. "Put your clothes on."

I would replay this scene over and over in my head later when I was questioned about his death and it would make it hard to focus on answering. "… remember who your friends are."

I didn't know what he meant, but I knew something about the way he said it wasn't right. I felt sick as he looked at me, naked. He licked his lips, gave a half smile, and left. I put my clothes on and went home without saying a word to Kara or anyone else. I still felt naked hours later and I couldn't stop thinking about the way he'd licked his lips.

8

One day, after the incident with Dante, when I walked in my classroom, my books were on the floor and the inside of my desk was a mess. Kara hadn't talked to me for a least a week and neither had anyone else. I'd been quietly going about my business in limbo, waiting for the silence to break at first, but then I'd gotten used to the not talking and was comfortable with it. I drew and sometimes listened or did my work. Sometimes not.

But now the silence was broken. My stuff had clearly been rifled through. My favorite eraser was missing as was my drawing notebook. *All my drawings, holy shit.* As the panic floated up, I saw a note. I unfolded it and read "bitch" in giant letters. It was signed by every girl in my class.

I knew who was behind it, but I wasn't sure the extent of what she told people. My ass prickled and started sweating and I was sick to my stomach.

Pale-faced, I asked, "Can I go to the bathroom?"

"Go!" Mr. Miller said, the alarm in his voice evidence that he thought I might throw up in the classroom.

In the bathroom my mind raced. I knew this was my fault for what happened with Kara and then the way her dad looked at me. Did she tell everyone I liked her brother? You didn't date your best friend's brother. If she had told people I liked Neil, the other kids would be on her side about it. Or worse...Oh my god, did she tell everyone what happened with her dad? What if she told them I did something with her dad? Worse, she probably told them I was a lesbian and that I'd tried to have sex with her. Now that I thought about it, maybe she told everyone I'd tried to kiss her or have sex with her or something and that she'd tried to stop me.

She was partly right. I had kissed her and more. I was disgusting. My ass kept sweating as I wished I could make myself throw up and feel better. Instead I sat on the toilet hoping as I shit that it would at least be diarrhea so I could go home. When I finished, my stomach was still all tied up in knots and I wondered how long I could stay there before someone would come looking for me. I wondered if it would be someone Kara had told and what they might do to me if they came to the bathroom to find me. I closed my eyes and tried counting but I couldn't get past twenty, even counting fast. I knew someone would come for me but I couldn't face going back to the classroom.

I stared at a heart-shape scratched into the bubble gum pink stall door with a paperclip. K + S = LOVE. Would people think I'd done that? That it meant Kara and Seffra? I could say I hadn't done it. I could say Kara had done it and then tell everyone she liked Sidney.

The idea terrified me. You didn't tell Kara's secrets. You just didn't. I hadn't even told anyone anything and look what was happening to me. Plus, no one would believe me anyway. They were probably going to call me a "lesbo" and I'd have no friends for the rest of...ever.

I pushed through the stall door and dragged my feet to the sink. I splashed cold water on my face and looked up. I was still pale. I could pretend to have gotten sick. Of course I could.

I felt better after thinking of a solution. I'd go to the nurse's office and tell her I'd thrown up. They'd send me home and this would be over.

Little did I know how much worse it would really get and how long it would be before it was over.

9

I didn't come back to school for days. It wasn't uncommon for me to skip a day here or there, but multiple days in a row was another story and I was up to three. I was on the border of how much you could miss without someone nosing around about why your mom hadn't called you in or asking too many questions about whether you'd been to the doctor and had gotten on medicine.

I didn't care though. My mom was in Chicago again, or somewhere anyway, and I couldn't convince myself to go back to school. I'd get upset thinking about my drawing notebook. That notebook had the entire year's worth of drawings. I'd taken it on trips and had done some of my best work in there.

Then I'd think of Kara and that afternoon in her house and I'd feel guilty and know it was all my fault anyway. I'd get panicked about Mr. Crosby telling my mom. Then I'd get panicked about where my mom might be and when she might be coming home.

So I stayed home. The third day I was home, I rifled through the bathroom and found my mom's stash of whiskey under the sink. I swallowed some and coughed. It dried out the back of my throat and burned but didn't taste too bad. Plus, the warmth broke up the pit in my belly and I felt numb. I took another sip then got an idea. I took Jell-O mix and licked my finger and dipped it in, then took a sip of the whiskey and then another lick of Jell-O mix. This seemed to launch me into myself. I was inside the pit now, the sprout long gone. I was completely calm and able to stare out at the world, thinking of nothing at all. It was a quiet ball of infinite nothing.

I sat on the couch staring at my hand and feeling my warm, numb belly and I didn't care about school. I didn't care about anything. I felt fine and I went to sleep.

I woke up, my head pounding to the beat of my mom slamming things around. The room was bright. She'd come back in the night but I hadn't heard her. I rushed and stashed the bottle back under the sink in the bathroom and peed.

"Where is my God *damned lighta*?"

I thought about faking sick and having her call me in but was too afraid they'd say something about the three previous days I'd also been missing. Plus, I could tell by the way she was slamming things around in her room and how often I heard "God damnit" that it would be no good staying home with her anyway. So I got up and started getting ready for school.

As I was getting dressed, my mom walked past. She caught sight of the usual mess on my floor and started yelling. She pushed me, hard. I fell and cowered, afraid of the additional rage I was sure was on its way. She kicked me pointedly in the ribs. "Ungrateful brat. Clean this shit up." She then left out the front door, slamming it on the way. Once I caught my breath, I lay in a puddle crying, scared, embarrassed. Somehow I was sure other people would know. They'd add it to the other shit they knew about me and I'd be ruined.

Surely anyone could see how worthless I was, how I deserved this punishment. After all, I knew my room was supposed to be clean. If I were better, less dirty, less gross, my mother'd take me with her. She wouldn't leave me and go to Chicago alone *or* with Mr. Crosby if I weren't such a piece of shit. I took deep breaths, tried to hurry the calming along. I knew if I didn't get to school on time, it'd be even more obvious that something was wrong with me. I absolutely did not want Mr. Miller in his irritated voice demanding an explanation when I walked in.

I prayed, "Uncle Phin, if you're here, please help me." Then I waited a minute to see if it'd worked. I breathed slowly, listening for him. After another moment, my breath regular again, I brushed myself off and headed toward the door. It was jammed. When she'd slammed it, she'd actually pulled the door *through* the frame. I stood thinking what to do. I *had* to go to school.

I went to my room, crawled out my window, and jumped the half-flight down to the ground. I ran and made it to school on time.

At school, my desk was still messy from the incident with Kara, but rather than clean it up, I reached around the mess and shoved loose papers further back into the metal compartment. I barely looked up all day and managed to avoid eye contact with everyone. Since I'd been out for three days, everyone chalked it up to me not feeling good and left me alone.

After school, I went to the shelter to walk the dogs.

"Missed you these last few days," the lady at the front desk said. I swallowed a lump and nodded.

"Yeah." I mumbled. "Can I take Sadie out?" My voice cracked as I said it.

"Oh," she whined, shaking her head, "I'm so sorry, but Sadie was adopted."

I hung my head as fat tears dripped onto the beige tiles at my feet. She put her hand on my shoulder and I gave in and cried. She guided me to the back cages and I buried my face in a Doberman. But it wasn't the same.

I took a basset hound named Belle out to walk once I'd calmed down. The cool air felt good against my cheeks but Belle kept tugging on the leash for all she was worth. Suddenly I hated that fucking dog. I really, deeply hated that little sausage shit. I kicked her and screamed, "*Heel.*" I kicked her again. I pulled and yelled, "You fucking idiot dog, *move.*" I kicked her again and again until I calmed down, until she whimpered, and I realized what I'd done.

It didn't help.

It was more proof of how fucking horrible I was. The pit remind-ed me it was still alive and well. The sprout had new growth as I hated every single thing about myself.

I arrived home that evening sweaty and tired, and the reality of what I was coming home to didn't touch me until I saw the front of our apartment. Dread flooded my chest. I still hadn't cleaned my room. Plus, how would I get in? The door had gone through the frame and couldn't be opened. I'd jumped to get out. But my mom would be expecting me to be home and my room clean regardless.

I examined the buildings. There were three buildings that faced into a courtyard in which the grass struggled to find enough sun to poke through the smooth clay soil. There were patches of success. They were emerald islands.

Our building was on the north end of the courtyard. There were indents, smooth and concave, between each brick. I stuck my fingers to the mortar, willing them to become Spidey-sticky. I tried holding on this way and my hands slid down. I stepped back and looked at the building. There was a brick ledge about an inch deep. I could put my foot on that, but then where would I reach for. The next ledge/win-dow/anything to hold onto was at least six feet above it. That wouldn't work. Desperate, I stepped up anyway.

I then braced myself against the side, holding the brick close to my chest, my face turned sideways. I jolt of terror traveled up my spine. This was a disaster waiting to happen. I leapt down.

I flopped to the ground, pounding my fists against the grass. I gave up and sat on front stoop. The sun had set now and I shivered against the cold, waiting for my mom to get home.

When she did, she had either completely forgotten the whole thing, or was doing an amazing job of pretending she had.

"How you doin' baby?" she asked, kissing me on the forehead. "How was your day?"

"Fine," I said looking down, afraid to make eye contact, afraid of ruining the mood.

"Seffra, baby, y' freezin'. Why aren't you inside?" she asked.

My mind raced, wondering what the best way to explain might be. "Um, the door's stuck." Suddenly irritated with her, I continued honestly, "It got stuck this morning when you slammed it and I had to crawl out my window. It won't open." Saying this was a risk.

A look of surprised skepticism crossed her brow as she headed to the door. She saw the door and laughed, an open-throated, full womanly laugh. "I can't believe it. You went out the window! Crazy girl." She chuckled, tousling my hair. "Let's get this kicked back in, huh, baby? You wanna help? You get to kick the door as hard as you can," she enticed.

I laughed with her as her mood caught and directed the energy in the room. The aggression, stress, fear, frustration, you name it, traveled out of us both as we kicked and kicked and eventually got the door on through again.

"You have any homework?"

"No, ma'am," I lied.

That evening we watched TV and the whole world was well again. Right before I went to sleep that night I said a prayer and thanked God for Uncle Phin.

Uncle Phin was nowhere to be found at school a few days later when Kara struck again.

I walked into class and saw immediately that my desk had been overturned and there were papers all around the floor. I turned it right side up and reached inside to see what was left. My drawing notebook had been returned only now the word BITCH was printed boldly across each one of my drawings in black permanent marker.

This time, I didn't even bother asking Mr. Miller to leave. I walked out the door and went home. I didn't know I wasn't coming back.

I'd been home for days. My mom was gone again and I didn't think it was to Chicago this time. Her eyes had been looking sunken and dark before she left and her mood had been consistently bad.

Home alone and drunk, I was eating a snack when there was a knock at the door. (My mom had gotten food stamps and decided to spend them on food instead of trading for something else this month.) I looked through the peephole and saw a lady with mousy brown hair and a suit on.

I opened the door, leaving the chain on and peered through the crack.

Not recognizing the woman, I asked, "who're you looking for," my eyebrows scrunched low.

"Hello, young lady. I'm with Social Services, and I'm here to see Linda Morgan. You must be Seffra," she said too sweetly.

"Yeah, you can leave. You're not welcome here," I said, shutting the door. She knocked again but I just yelled, "Catch the message lady!" I bragged to myself under my breath, *I told her.*

My mother had always said she wanted nothing to do with the Social Services people. When she talked about the social worker that had come when she was pregnant with me, she'd said, "That's how you have to handle those people. You have to let them know and show 'em the door. I let them *know* in Georgia. I'd be damned if I let some social services people take my daughter." So I did exactly what she'd told me. I'd protected us. I'd keep us together just like my mom had.

After five days of not bothering to go to school and my mom still gone, Mr. Jackson, the principal, came by the house. He knocked and I answered.

"Is your mom around?" he asked. "I tried to call but it seems we have the wrong number listed or something. The number was disconnected."

"Um, no. She's not here right now." I was nervous; what was he doing here? "She went to the store, to get medicine for me," I blurted out stupidly. I knew it'd be bad if he figured out how long she'd been gone.

He looked past me into our apartment. The entryway didn't get much light. I stared at the welcome mat and thought I saw a cockroach flit past. I rubbed my eyes. The light was out in the hallway and it was hard to see.

"Medicine huh? I'm glad to hear you've seen a doctor and will be getting better soon. A trip to the pharmacy shouldn't take too long. I'll wait then." His voice bounced off the empty walls and up the stairwell.

Shit, shit, shit. What should I do now?

"She might not come straight home. I think she had some other errands to run too," I said, trying to figure out how to get him to leave. "I'm not sure."

"Well, I'll wait for a bit if you don't mind and if it gets too late, I'll leave her a note and skip on home."

"Um—" I said. "—I'm not sure my mom would want me to let you in the house since she doesn't know you. Maybe I better come out." I lowered my voice. "The house is kind of a mess."

"Ahhh," he said with a large understanding nod. "Of course."

Our footsteps echoed loudly as we stepped down the couple of stairs and into the courtyard. There were two aluminum lawn chairs without too many tears in the nylon weaving so we sat down on the steps.

I didn't know which would be worse: if she came home, or if she didn't. I decided not coming home was better. Hopefully he'd just think she was busy and that'd be that.

I made idle and stupid comments, hoping to fill the vast and uncomfortable space made when your principal, who is supposed to live in an office in the school and nowhere else, comes over to your house, which is supposed to be for non-school things. She never came home, thankfully, and he left after a bit, seemingly unconcerned.

He left a note.

"Dear Ms. Morgan-

I stopped by to check on Seffra. We've been worried about her. Let us know if there's any way the school can help."

He signed it and left his numbers, both at the school and his home phone number. If *that* isn't rude. *Sorry your phone's disconnected, but look! You can reach me on one of two phones. Two!*

My mom came home in the middle of the night. She came in and went straight to bed. She was still sleeping when I left for school the next morning.

I walked out the front door, took a right and headed for school. But a block or so into my walk, I started worrying about what school would say. They'd certainly ask about the note and be wondering when they'd hear from my mother. It was getting harder and harder to hold my shit together and I couldn't handle it if I broke down at school. Not in front of Kara and the other kids. I couldn't face it if they called me "lesbo" or messed with me again.

So I said screw it and went to Tower Grove Park. I could relax there and let the stuff with Kara go. I could breathe.

I wandered past one of the manmade ponds. It had white pillars that stood twenty feet tall announcing a platform where ladies in the 1919 World's Fair would have stepped with dainty feet to have their picture taken. Now there were vines trying to pull that same platform into the algae-filled waters. I glanced over and saw Boogie. I immediately smiled and headed over to say hi.

Boogie was this raggedy guy who brought a milk crate everywhere he went so he could flip it upside down, stand on it, and proselytize. I'd first seen him when my mom took me to the library when I was six, but I didn't know him yet then. Boogie's favorite thing was to rhyme his sermons. When he was 'feelin' the spirit movin'' he'd be rhyming away, wiggling his hips and jerking around in his own form of a dance. He'd really dance: thus the name Boogie.

By now I knew him pretty well from skipping school and playing in the park.

Sometimes he had a whole audience of people listening to him and they'd drop money in his hat. But today, he didn't really have much of an audience, so he was sitting on his crate looking bored and dirty. On days when he was just hanging out like this, I'd listen to what he had to say about God, or just strike up a conversation. He loved a good joke so I stopped off to tell him my latest.

"What's the difference between chopped beef and pea soup? Give up? Everyone can chop beef, but not everyone can pee soup!"

He laughed and I moved on. I wasn't in the mood to listen to a sermon anymore than he was to give one.

I sat under a tree for a while and tried to take a nap. But then I heard thunder announcing impending spring showers. Defeated, I decided to go home. Maybe my mom was still sleeping and wouldn't notice that I was two and half hours early.

I told my mom we'd had a half-day of school when I got home and she didn't question it. The walk and the time with Boogie had cheered me up and school and my guilt and insecurities felt miles away.

In our apartment, the floor plan was open in the front. Beyond the living area, the shotgun style apartment continued straight back with bedrooms and bathroom along the hallway. The open living area had a counter and stove along the inside wall and the sink and another counter along the outside wall. Our kitchen table was in the center and beyond it was the living room with our ratty couch. My mother sat with a tumbler in her hand and a cigarette between her fingers at the kitchen table and I stood at the stove making late afternoon dinner: Lipton noodles and sauce and frozen vegetables. I was proud of myself.

I was chatting away about the dog walking and the book I was reading and music I liked, and on and on. My mom was buzzed, but sappy drunk. I never liked any of her styles when she was drunk, but I *almost* liked sappy drunk. It meant she would be repeating herself and giving excessively slobbery kisses and that day especially I could deal with extra kisses. If I'd only known, I would have grabbed hold and never told her.

I was energetically fueled by her attention and the way it stripped away all the guilt and hatred of the kids at school. All I needed was more of my mom and me together. But I didn't know that it could be so healing then.

I wore an oven mitt on my hand and carried the steamy pot over to the table and set it down. I spooned some noodles onto white Corningware plates and then sat down. I picked up my fork and started eating, still chattering away.

"Oh hey, Ma, I forgot to tell you that a lady from Social Services came by the other day," I said lightly. "I did just what you did though. I told her she wasn't welcome and didn't let her in," I continued, proudly.

The blow that followed was so swift and unexpected it knocked me *and* my fork across the room. A single curled noodle lay in a puddle of speckled splash on the linoleum.

"What in God's *name*!" she screamed. "Are you retarded?! Jesus, what kind of idiot child am I raisin'?" She continued, "Why didn't you *tell me*?!"

I barely noticed the sting of the cigarette going out against my skin.

"I just did," I said through snot. I cried uncontrollably, paralyzed on the floor.

"You think you're smart, dontcha?"

Accusing me of thinking I was smart only fueled her fury and she grabbed me by the arm. She looked at me, disgusted, her upper lip curled. She dragged me to my room and threw me in.

She slammed the door. Her yell came muffled through the door. *"You can come out when you grow a few damned brain cells."*

I cried and cried. I didn't even know what to actually be scared of. Was my mom going to give me away because of how stupid I was? Would I be grounded? When would I be allowed out of my room? And oh, how I wanted to go back and take the whole thing back. I would go back and not tell my mom. No, wait, I'd go back and pretend to have never been home at all when that bitch came over. Why couldn't people just leave us alone? We were fine if they'd just leave us alone. I hyperventilated and cried myself to sleep.

When I woke up the next morning I slowly, quietly crept to the bathroom to pee and see about the damage to my face from the night before. After all, maybe the social worker would come back and I wanted to make sure to fix myself up as best as I could before that happened.

I surveyed the condition of my face. My eyes were puffy and my cheek was red and swollen, but nothing too serious. I took a cold washcloth and let it sit on my closed eyes and thought what to do. I needed to ice my cheek but was worried about a trip to the kitchen. I wasn't supposed to leave my room until my mom said it was okay. The bathroom was one thing - I really had to pee - but sometimes she even got mad about that. The kitchen was a pretty big risk. But if I didn't ice my cheek, it was likely to get worse and I could end up with a big bruise.

I sat in the bathroom listening for sounds in the house. Happy sounds, busy sounds, abrupt slamming of pan sounds, anything that might help me make a decision. All was quiet. Eerily quiet. I decided to risk it.

I tiptoed across the slanted tile floor to the kitchen, glancing around for signs of my mom and her mood. The pot of dinner and our dishes sat on the table, a skin of congealed sauce over the top. I cried quietly, looking at our spoiled dinner and my stomach growled.

I wiped my eyes and got a bag of frozen peas out of the freezer. Pea soup, I suddenly thought, and smiled. Dang, that's a funny joke. I took the peas to my room, where I thought I'd be safer. Hopefully my mom wouldn't have heard me and I could pretend like I'd been there all along the way I was supposed to be.

I iced my face for a while, then slid the bag under my bed for safe keeping. I found a notepad and started drawing. I tried a flower and found it too hard and also not right for my mood. I stared out the window for a long time, blurring my vision, then bringing it into focus again. I pushed on my eyelids to make the sparkles flash before my eyes, then opened them suddenly surveying the scene in the sparkling room. I reached my hand up and fiddled with my necklace. The broken glass piece from my mom calmed me. The wall I focused on had a window. There was a single point where something must've hit it and the cracks sprayed out from there. I picked up my pad and pencil and started drawing. I was lost for a long time in the task, not hearing anything around me. I looked at it when I was finished.

It was the wall, complete with shading for the stains and peeling plaster near the corner by the ceiling. In the middle of my picture was the window. I included the sheet that hung from above the window and was blowing to the right, as well as a ray of sun that shone into the cracked pane and splintered. It wasn't perfect, but it wasn't bad.

Seconds after I finished my rendering, my mom opened the door.

"You're going to stay with the Crosbys' for a while. Just 'til I figure out what to do." She paused. "Pack y' things."

"But, but…" I stammered.

"I've got a heavy load on my mind and now that there's a Goddamn social worker involved, I've got to figure what to do."

My stomach filled with bile and my mind turned red. "No Mom, please. Can't I stay here? No one'll know. I won't answer the door or even leave to go to school. I'll be good, please. Just don't make me go to the Crosbys'," I begged.

"What on earth? I thought you'd be happy to go to the Crosbys'. What's goin' on?" My mom stopped and grabbed my face, her thumb and index fingers pressing into my cheeks as she searched my face. She released me brusquely. "Never mind, it doesn't matter. You girls are gonna have t' work out whatever it is that's goin' on between you."

I begged and cried. I tried to convince her of how mean Kara was being but she blamed me for the problems and I didn't dare tell her about what I was really worried about. I was too ashamed. I begged to be allowed to stay home.

"You can't stay here. It might be a while. There's nowhere else to take you. You'll have to go," she explained.

She continued, "C'mon Seffra, don't make this difficult. This is your fault anyway. Don't make me the bad guy here." She pronounced here as though it had two syllables and carried out the last in that drawl of hers.

Anything would be better than going there. I was terrified to see Kara again. Not to mention how I felt about Mr. Crosby but there was no getting out of it.

I hid my drawing between the mattresses and grabbed my favorite Swiss army knife and some other odds and ends a girl can't be without, like my makeup and my shower shoes, and we headed out. She held car keys and beeped an alarm button.

I wondered whose fancy car but didn't dare ask. I also wondered why we'd need a car. We usually walked to Kara's.

"Where are we going, Mama?" I asked cautiously.

"Dante's got a place he can stash you in West County."

That's why we needed the car.

West County was far. We didn't spend much time there. It was filled with curving roads and cul-de-sacs. The homes were held up by columns in front and they boasted *two*-car garages. I couldn't imagine what Dante Crosby could be doing out there. He was kind of a loser. And West County was full of rich people.

Dante Crosby didn't belong in West County. He drank heavily whether he was hanging out with my mom or not, but definitely if he was hanging out with her. He had huge forearms from doing machine work. He'd been in the military but got kicked out for insubordination. Now he worked odd jobs and when he wasn't otherwise engaged he picked on his kids. I couldn't imagine what my mother saw in him. He didn't seem nearly fun enough, or rich enough, or, well, good enough for my mom. True, she had her flaws, but she was stylish, beautiful, and clever. He was raunchy, drunk, and mean.

When we got to the house, I thought seriously about stiffly placing my arms and legs against the doorframe and refusing to enter the house. Maybe I could stand my ground and be immovable.

But my mom gave me a look that said I wouldn't see another day if I did. So I went in.

Dante kissed my mom on one cheek and smacked her on the other. A tacky move I couldn't believe she tolerated. But she smiled coyly and batted her eyelashes. Yech.

The house was a three-bedroom ranch-style brick home with two separate living areas. Only one of them had furniture, and then only a couch, a TV, an end table, and a scuffed-up coffee table. The couch turned out to be a sofa bed. Dante showed me how to open it up and said I could put my stuff in a nightstand that doubled as an end table. I didn't have a lot so the two drawers would work fine. The kitchen turned out to be completely empty. Dante caught me looking in the cabinets.

"Mind your business, girl, and stay outa here."

I wasn't sure what this would mean for eating but clearly the kitchen was used to house something other than food that I thankfully hadn't stumbled upon. It must've been a stash-house.

I spent two days obsessing about where Kara and her brothers might be and whether I'd see them. Dante and I didn't speak. He was barely there. I didn't know when I'd hear from my mom but didn't dare bring it up with Dante. I didn't want to interact with him more than I absolutely had to. I didn't want to draw attention to my existence. Dante grunted at me to help myself after returning from the grocery store with frozen pizzas and TV dinners. He said to stay away from the cupboards but the deep freezer was where I could get food. Other than eating, I watched TV or drew. Or I thought about Kara.

I wasn't pissed at her anymore about the kids at school or my drawing notebook. I was just lonely. Kara had been my friend for a long time and I missed her. I was scared she was still mad at me and even though that made me a little angry because of how wrong she obviously would be to hold a grudge, I was also afraid of her grudges and missed my friend. I was ashamed of myself for not staying mad like I should too though. I knew I shouldn't want a friend who treated me like she had, but I did.

Dante moved the kids out to the county a few days later. They didn't make eye contact or say anything so I didn't either. They took the bedrooms and I stayed out of the way. I knew if Kara didn't pretend like nothing had happened I should steer clear.

And at first I did steer clear but then one day we were all watching TV in the same room and then the boys left to go hang out at the neighborhood school and play some football but Kara stayed behind and suddenly it was just the two of us.

We avoided talking for a bit but then Kara broke the silence.

"Turn it up, wouldya?"

I took this as my opening, gathering my courage. "Is there anything to do around here?"

"You and your whore mom never seem to have trouble finding things to do," was all she said before leaving the room.

It had been days and I wanted to know what my mom had planned. I was running out of patience with waiting to hear what was going on. I knew she'd keep us together somehow but wanted to know details. How long would it be? Where were we going? What was the plan? She hadn't called though and even if she did, I wouldn't dare ask.

I figured out where the library was, and was careful to go when schools would be out so the librarian wouldn't suspect anything. School was ending in a month so it wouldn't be long before I didn't have to worry about it anyway. I checked out drawing books and mysteries.

I made myself a fort by the creek out of two big boards I found by someone's garage and a discarded, torn tarp. Over time I added things to it to make it cozier: a coffee can with sand that I put a candle in for light if I went late at night; a long smooth board and the padding from a torn comforter made a nice spot to lounge, and other things. I taped up pictures of Madonna and other stars I cut out of magazines, and brought a decent blanket I pilfered from a trashcan.

One guy, about five blocks away had a treasure trove of crap in his yard so I climbed over the privacy fence to pilfer what I could. But he caught me and yelled through a window, "I've got a shot gun and I'ma give you to the counta five before I go an git it." I scrambled back over empty-handed and never went back.

I'd been at the Crosby crash pad for nearly three weeks when I realized I didn't have to do any chores. The other kids did. Kara had kitchen duties mostly. Neil had to do yard stuff and Marcello had to take care of the other indoor cleaning and take the trash out. But after two weeks, Marcello had had enough and demanded I do my share.

"If she's gonna live here, she should have to do chores, too!" he complained. "She shouldn't get no free ride! She don't pay rent or nothin'."

Dante stopped him short. "She's doin' plenty. You leave her and don't you worry about it."

What was I doing? I read books and stayed silent nearly all the time. I was trying my hardest to un-exist. I didn't *do* anything. Marcello slumped over in defeat and stomped down the hall to his room. I stared at the brown carpet.

Kara got a twisted grin on her face. "You missed a call while you were gone today."

"I did? Was it my mom? What'd she say? Did she leave a number so I can call her back?"

"No, stupid, it wasn't your mom. But it *was* the recording from the jail where your mom's at," she laughed.

Now I was really mad. "No she's not. *She's* too smart for jail." I narrowed my gaze and glared at her while I said it. It was a dig on Kara because her family had tons of people who'd gone to jail, including Dante.

"Kara, go to your room. Seffra, it wasn't your mom." He glared at Kara. "Don't *make* me show you both how to behave," he threatened.

Kara had her back to her dad now as she headed after Marcello down the hall to her own room. She rolled her eyes and stuck her tongue out at me.

"Is my mom really in jail?" I knew I shouldn't talk; I shouldn't have said anything at all. I should have just waited and kept my ears open. But I had to know. Maybe my mom needed my help. Not that I had any idea how to help her, but it was my job to make sure someone did.

"Don't let Kara get to you. She's trying to rattle your cage," was all he said.

At first that was enough and I went back to the sleeper sofa and reading my mystery. I didn't want to go to my fort. I wanted my mom to call. What if I missed it when my mom really did call? What if Kara answered and then never told me about it?

What if Kara hadn't been lying at all and my mom really had called collect from jail? When I thought back, Dante hadn't actually told me that she *wasn't* in jail. At bedtime I was still thinking about the earlier conversation and wondering about my mom. I replayed everything that was said all the way back to Marcello getting mad that I didn't have to do chores and Dante saying I did plenty. Maybe he felt sorry for me because my mom really was in jail. But that seemed unlikely.

Later on that night I found out what the plenty was that I was doing. Mr. Crosby crept into the living room around three when the bar closed. I woke to hear the squeak of the mattress and froze.

He smelled to high-heaven of whiskey. It wasn't just his breath either. It was his skin. It emitted this awful odor like something in him was putrefying or fermenting from within or maybe both. I gagged.

"You do plenty now, dontcha girl?" he breathed. I gagged again. I was so revolted I didn't have time to panic.

"Mmmm, you's a good girl, aintcha? Prolly a virgin too…mmm." His breath was hot as he drew out the words.

He reached his index finger out and caressed my arm and I could feel the jagged edges and grooves of his cracked, rough skin, workman's hands. My body was being pulled toward the center of the bed where his substantial size weighed the bed down.

I felt his lips against my arm and the bed rocking and swaying slightly, rhythmically. His breathing turned heavier and deeper, then faster.

I was trying to keep still, pretend to be sleeping, just not move and have it not be happening.

Oh god, oh god, oh god. I couldn't keep up the frozen act anymore. The smell of his breath, and the feel of his saliva on my arm were getting to me.

"I'm gonna be sick, Mr. Crosby," I said getting up and running to the bathroom. And I was. I puked several times. Then I got up and began rinsing my mouth out. I splashed water on my face to collect myself.

I sat down, cross-legged on the cold tile floor enjoying the chill against my bare legs. Then suddenly, I had. To. Get. OUT.

So I scrambled through the window without really considering the consequences of what I was doing. In the cold and dark and in my pajamas now, I was suddenly aware of my body and the outdoors. My toes grew colder and the frost where I stood, melted, steam floating up my legs. The pins and needles felt good in my toes and the puffs of steam from my mouth seemed reassuring. Still I knew I couldn't just stand there. I thought where to go: my fort. It was the only place no one knew about where I would be safe until morning.

I strained my eyes in the dark, vigilant for sticks and glass I might step on as well as people since I needed to avoid detection. I stepped carefully. The sticks I found were damp and did not snap underfoot. I silently, slowly, painstakingly made it to the fort where I lit my candle. I took a deep breath and let it out. I blew out the candle, worrying someone would see me. I wrapped my pajamas around me as well as a blanket and lay down on my makeshift reading pad. I clutched my Swiss army knife tightly in my right hand and lay on my left side listening hard. I began to shake violently. Then suddenly, I couldn't keep my eyes open. Exhaustion overtook me and I slept.

When I woke up, my hand was cramped from how tightly I'd clutched the knife, even in my deepest sleep. I set it down and stared at it while kneading the meat of my hand. I needed to start planning. I knew my mom wouldn't stand for Dante touching me. She'd told me as much. I didn't care what he told my mom anymore, it didn't matter. I only had to get to her so I could tell her about him. The real him. Which meant finding a way home. And to get home, I'd need clothes.

I'd have to head back to the house to get clothes. I wasn't sure what else to do. I hadn't grabbed any of my stuff and I was practically in the middle of nowhere, wearing my pajamas. I knew I could make my way back to the city by bus but if I was going to take the bus back home to find my mom, I'd at least need to be wearing clothes.

I worried about going to the front door since I was likely to be seen by one of the perfect suburbanites scratching behind the ear of a perfect golden retriever who'd just fetched their perfect fucking newspaper. The fort was in the ravine that lay creek-side behind the house. So I snuck to the back door and tried the chipped chrome handle. It turned and I went in.

I'd been afraid of basements since I was little and the back door led into the basement of the house so I'd never gone that way until now. The basement was dirty. Filled with dust and cobwebs and giant black bugs that abruptly leapt three-feet in the air, the basement floor was unfinished and littered with random household crap: a red plastic bucket with an inch of dirty unknown liquid, rusted wrenches and screw drivers in an open wooden toolbox on the floor, and wooden steps to the upstairs. I hated my naked feet touching the cold damp surface and sprint-tiptoed across it to the stairs.

I silently opened the door and peered through the house. I didn't see any sign of Kara and her brothers but Dante was passed out on the couch next to my stuff. I couldn't risk it. So I went to Kara's room. She was asleep but had always been a hard sleeper so I snuck in, stole clothes, and snuck out as fast as I could.

I was usually good at stealing. I did it when I was bored or wanted something, or when my mom was gone and I needed to eat. Also, sometimes I just did it and didn't know why. I'd learned, though, never to steal from places you frequented. You didn't steal from people you knew or places you went all the time. Whenever I broke these rules or lifted stuff I didn't really need, I seemed to get caught. I'd get a guilty, peppery feeling in my gut and if I ignored it, I got caught. Every time.

Once when I ignored the warning feeling and the rules, I got caught shoplifting some makeup from the drug store down the street. My mom came to pick me up and extended a slender wrist. The officer actually took it and kissed her hand.

"Lord, I don't know what I'm gonna do with this girl." She exhaled and reached her index finger under her sunglasses to wipe away a fake tear.

"We live right around the cornah if you don't mind coming by, I'd offer you something to drink and we can sort this out. I wouldn't bother you, it's just, we've got a handyman comin' by today and I don't want to miss him. Bein' a single mother an' all, I need to take whatever help I can get!"

The officer came home with us and the trouble over the shoplifting was long forgotten by the time he left, as was the handyman who had mysteriously never shown.

But after the cop left, the strikes that fell on my face and back as I got a reminder of the rules about not stealing were anything but those of a gentle, helpless single mother.

"Don't you bring the law into this house. And don't you *dare* steal from the corna store where you live, idiot-girl." She hissed *idiot-girl* again as she struck me over and over.

But I didn't have a choice now. I had to have some clothes and Kara's were the only option I was willing to risk. They'd be too big but hopefully it wouldn't be noticeable. So I ignored the feeling.

I tucked a shirt into jeans and used a belt to hold them up, hoping it would be enough and headed out the door for the best place to go to get information.

At the library, I told the woman at the counter that I was working on a project for my church youth group. The youth group was supposed to figure out all the details for a trip into the city to serve a dinner to the homeless. I was in charge of the transportation. She bought it, and helped me figure out how to take the bus into the city. The bus fare with all the transfers and everything would run me just over two bucks and it'd take an hour to get to the south side. That wasn't too bad, but I didn't have *any* money so even coming up with a couple dollars was going to be hard.

The first bus of the day was at 5:05 a.m. and they ran hourly after that until 7:05 p.m. The only question was: how would I get the money?

The suburbs aren't a good place to beg for it. You can pull that off in a city, but in suburbs people freak out about that sort of thing and call the cops. At least that's what I thought they'd do. And I wasn't willing to risk it. I thought of the book *Where the Red Fern Grows*. The boy in that book digs up worms and sells them as bait, saving every penny he can get his hands on. While there was a creek to play around, this wasn't some rural town. I couldn't sell bait. What could I do? Lemonade stand? Nah, that's crap and doesn't get you money. Slingin'? Too tough in the yuppie preppy suburbs. I'd have to steal it.

Because of the rush, I knew I'd have to steal it from one of the stores close to the house. I thought of the rules about not stealing too close to where you live and decided the rule didn't apply because I really lived in the city with my mom.

I thought of the different stores where I could go to steal. The grocery store? Wait, even better: the drug store. People in the drug store were always either not feeling good or fighting with their kids about what they didn't want to buy for them. They were distracted and that would make them easy targets.

So, I had the place. Now I needed a cover. What would I be doing while I was waiting for the person to steal from? It needed to be something inconspicuous that nobody'd care about.

Finally it came to me: reading. Of course, nobody ever bothers a little girl reading. I could go grab a book or magazine from the shelf and sit in the chairs by the pharmacy counter and wait for a good purse to come along. It was perfect.

Since the hay fever was so bad that year, the drug store was really busy. And that was good because it meant that there was bustle and crowds, which makes stealing easier since there's more cover. Also, in 1991, the only over-the-counter meds for allergies made people pretty drowsy. So people were really out of it on over-the-counter medicine. Their eyes were puffy. They were unfocussed. It was great.

I found a kid's magazine and sat down to wait. I read a little, so I'd have something to say if anyone asked me what I was reading, and eyed the store layout. The pharmacists' counter was in front of me but the pharmacists themselves went a ways back to fill prescriptions and call in requests. They were frequently away from the counter to do these things so there'd be time with no employees looking. There were three people in line with hay fever, a man in a cast picking up crutches, and one lady with a not readily visible problem. There was a large woman sitting in the seat next to me. She was so big she was sort of leaking over onto my seat. Her purse was right next to me. It was practically touching me.

I looked slyly over my magazine figuring out when I would make my move. I'd have to be quick and I'd need some sort of distraction to get into her purse without her knowing. I decided I'd sneeze and drop my magazine. Hopefully she'd pick it up and while she was doing that, I'd get into her purse. I gathered my courage. But as I was about to "sneeze," they called her name and she got up to fetch her prescription. It made me jittery. The I'm-gonna-get-caught feeling crept up. I pushed it down.

Shit. *Calm down, there will be other chances,* I told myself. But I was worried. Somehow I thought when I was planning all this, it would be fine to stay in the store all morning, even all day if I needed to, but now sitting there I realized this was nothing like the library and I had a limited amount of time sitting there before it would be suspicious. I considered stealing at the library but dismissed that idea immediately. I'd always loved going to the library, since I was a little girl. They gave away books for free and told you about all the best ones and had story times where they read to kids with voices and props. Libraries were filled with nice ladies who answered any question you had without ever making you feel stupid. I absolutely could not steal at the library. I breathed and waited.

The next person who sat down was a blind old lady. She had the dog and everything. I couldn't steal from her. I thought she'd understand if I did, but I couldn't bring myself to do it. *Move lady,* I thought. *I need to get some money and I can't get it from you.*

Finally, a man sat down. He was practically unconscious from his allergy medicine; at least I think that's what was making him like that. *And* he had pulled his wallet out of his pocket and was sitting there waiting with it in his lap. He leaned his head back and started to doze off. I watched, and saw that the coast was clear, no one was watching. So I gently pulled at a twenty-dollar bill. When I'd almost gotten it out he stirred. I let go briefly, then reached out again. Just as I did, a woman started banging her fist on the counter.

"Miss, Miss. Can't a person get any help around here!" she exclaimed in a nasal, rude voice.

I took the chance and tugged quickly. The man startled awake but assumed it was the lady's bitching that woke him. He sniffled, wiped his face for drool, adjusted his position and went back to dozing.

I'd done it! I got up, set the magazine down, and headed for the door. Yes!! I was going home!

Right at the door, a clerk tapped me on the shoulder.

Shit.

"Young lady. Don't you suppose you should put things back where you found them?" he said, sweeping his arm out, broadly gesturing across the store.

My sweat turned cold and covered my palms. "Huh?" I asked, trying to sound innocent. I tried following his gaze but didn't understand.

He cocked his head to one side, not buying it.

I looked down.

"The magazine. You should really buy it, not come in here and read it for free and then leave it on a chair by pharmacy. Don't you think?"

You've got to be kidding me. "Yes sir. I'm sorry. I was bored waiting for my dad to get his medicine," I lied, looking from side to side and lowering my voice. "Please don't tell him," I added for good measure.

"I'll let it go this time. But next time I'm going to make you pay for that, missy."

"Yes sir," I said handing him the magazine and looking down.

"Good. I'm glad you learned your lesson."

Whew. And I was on my way home again.

Unconsciously, I reached my hand for the necklace my mother had given me. But it wasn't there. I must've taken it off at the Crosbys'. My heart sunk. I would have to go back. Again.

I knew it was a risk but I could not bear to leave that necklace behind. I just couldn't.

Still, I wasn't excited about going back to the crash pad. Since I had money and didn't really want to go yet, I crossed the busy cement intersection at the light and headed over to Taco Bell to eat and kill a little time and gather some courage before going back.

I tasted the greasy spice in my mouth and my belly was full. When I got back to the house, the kids were gone but Dante was home and up now.

"Hey there, Seff," he said cheerily.

I raised my eyebrows and looked at him, dumbfounded.

He was sitting at the kitchen table and took a bite of toast and a swig of his coffee. I smelled the burnt toast and his hangover. "Hair of the dog, eh?" he said, pointing at his mug and smiling. There was a fifth of Jim Beam on the table next to him empty.

71

"Some night I had last night. I don't remember a thing." He looked pointedly at me.

I waited, my mouth turning sour, suddenly old, my stomach beginning to churn. My necklace lay on the table next to the empty bottle. I stole a glance at it. He rapped his knuckles once and stood up.

"Getting ready to go get your mom and go to Chicago for a coupla days." He gestured toward a black duffle bag by the door. "By the way, your mom told me about that dog you liked so much and I adopted it for you. It's at a friend's house and I'll pick it up for you on my way back into town." His lips curled back in a fake smile that revealed too many teeth.

"Sadie?" I asked. "But, when?"

"Right before you got here." He paused. "You got anything you want me to tell your mother?"

My chest felt hollowed out, emptied of blood and refilled with a pulsing sludge. I shook my head and left my hair hanging in my face.

"Good. Then that dog should be fine until I get back." He paused and a beat passed.

"But, if you had something to say…" he trailed off. Then he shook his head. "Well, I'm sure she'll be fine as long as you remember who your friends are."

That again.

Then he sneered and tossed my necklace to me. "Hey, I think this is yours." He grabbed his duffle bag and walked out of the room.

I'd caught the necklace and stood there holding it to my chest a long while, willing the necklace to stop my racing heartbeat.

What was I going to do? Now my mother was leaving for Chicago with him and I wouldn't be able to sneak into the city to tell her because she'd be gone. And, I had to make sure Sadie was safe. I knew he was threatening me with Sadie. He had her at a friend's house and was going to hurt her if I told. I wasn't stupid. I knew what he was telling me. Why had it all gotten so complicated? I didn't know what to do about any of my problems. But at least I had a little bit of time while they'd be gone. I fiddled with the glass piece on its chain and thought how much I wanted to be back with my mom again. She'd know what to do.

10

Dante shuffled around from his bedroom to the bathroom and back, slamming things around. He couldn't find his keys to leave. I stood dumbfounded for a while, trying not to think. I tried to just stand there and be.

Giving in, I sat down on the couch and listened. I heard my heart in my ears. It thudded and the noise calmed me. I took deep breaths and listened to the thudding. Eventually, my heartbeat slowed and became regular again.

Then Kara walked in. "What. The. Fuck?" she said and slapped me right across the face. "Take off my clothes, you fucking lesbo whore!" She screamed and grabbed the bottom of the shirt I was wearing.

I was scared but even in my fear, I still thought, *She did call me a lesbo to the other kids at school. That's how she did it. That's how she turned them against me.* Where she held onto me by her own shirt audibly tore in her hands and Dante came in.

"What's going on?"

"That fucking whore *stole my clothes!*" She was raging now but his thick hand held her back from clawing me apart.

"Simmer down," he said but she didn't stop. She kept trying to attack me until he finally slammed her into a chair and said right into her face, "I *said* simmer down!" His teeth were clenched and the words spit their way through his teeth, saliva-marinated threats.

She panted for a moment, her breath slowing as she sat slumped over, glaring at the floor.

"You got plenty-a clothes, little girl. Stop worrying about this one—" he gestured toward me "—and go on back to your room."

She stomped down the hall, then turned and glared over her shoulder but the fight was out of her now.

"You two are gonna have to figure this out," he added. Then he followed her back and I heard him through the open door. "I'm going to Chicago. You leave that Morgan girl alone, hear?"

I wasn't sure whether to be more afraid of Dante staying or leaving. Once he left there was no telling how it would be when I was outnumbered by the Crosby kids. But I didn't want him to stay and attack me again either. Plus, now the money I'd stolen would have to last longer. I was planning to leave right away, but now it'd probably be three days before they'd be back and I'd need a couple bucks for bus fare. I'd splurged at Taco Bell already so only had $14 left for food for three days. I could swing that.

I went to the grocery store and paid for some Ramen noodles and also stole a couple of Snickers, a three-stick pack of lip balm, and a pack of gum just because. Stealing was easy. And it made me feel confident, like I was in control, like I could have whatever I wanted. I reached my hand in my pocket and fingered the lip balm all the way back to the house.

Once I was back, I tried to quietly disappear. I longed to be alone but I was out of luck because the boys were around. Thankfully, Kara holed up somewhere and I didn't see her for a while. Neil offered to play cards with me and I wanted to. I really wanted to. But I said no and went back to reading a book I'd lifted from the library, rationalizing that I'd have checked it out except I couldn't get a card without a parent and I'd promised myself I'd return it just as though I'd borrowed it just without a card.

That weekend, I lay around thinking, playing the eye games, eating Ramen, but the clock barely moved. Then Saturday afternoon Marcello 'found' a bike. We all went outside and the Crosby kids took turns riding it. I followed them outside to watch. Kara occasionally glared my way but mostly ignored me. Marcello had taken his turns and gotten bored already and now Neil was riding around.

Kara glared at me again.

"What is your problem? I'm sorry about the clothes, but I didn't have anything to wear and your dad's right. You've got plenty of clothes!"

Kara got close. She stared right into my face, her face pinched with anger. "You. You shut your mouth. You and your whole damned family do nothing but take from us. Your mom took my mom. You fucked my brother and now you have the nerve to think this is about some clothes? You're a whore just like your mom and I want you to stay away from us."

I had no idea what to say to her. I didn't know what she was talking about. How had my mom taken her mom away? Her mom died in a drunk driving accident. My mom hadn't even been there.

"What are you talking about? I didn't fuck your brother? Ew. I don't even know which brother you're talking about. I've never had sex with anyone."

But then I did. It had to have been Neil. He would have lied and said I did. That was why she started messing with me.

Neil was showing off by doing wheelies and riding with no hands. I wanted to crush him. I wanted to push the bike over while he rode around all cocky with no hands. But I didn't do anything. I stood there like an idiot until they went in a minute later.

Then, I rode the bike around for an hour or so, and thought about the possibility of riding the bike home to the city. I could stay at my own apartment where I was safe and didn't have to worry about wanting to beat the shit out of Neil or Kara's wrath or Dante's disgusting return, or what Kara was saying about my mother and her mother. With the money I saved on bus fare, I could buy more food if my mom and Dante were gone more than three days. But I didn't know if I could ride that far and I was worried about getting lost. So I gave up the idea of going back to the city for the time being.

I fantasized about going back to the store and graciously apologizing for the items I'd "accidentally" stolen and paying for them. The fantasy eased my guilt but I wasn't going to do it. Still, thinking about going back and paying was better than outright stealing. I peeled back the paper on my Snickers and took a slow luxurious bite.

Saturday night we all sat around watching TV. I sat in the corner and hoped they'd leave me alone.

Neil was on the floor with a pillow and Marcello and Kara took either end of the couch, while I sat in the corner against the wall with my knees tucked up, hoping no one would say anything to me. I was furious about Neil's lie but didn't know what to do about it and was in the middle of seething and doing nothing.

"There's nothing on TV. We should *do* something," Neil complained.

"Like what?" Marcello asked, leaning his back against the couch, hard.

"I know. We could tie Seffra up and draw all over her face," Kara replied, smiling.

Neil smiled too and tossed the pillow up onto the couch, sitting up. That mischievous smile sent a tingle through me and I turned away to avoid killing him or worse, smiling too. They were talking about drawing on my face. He'd said he had sex with me. What the fuck was wrong with me that I wanted to smile?

"We'd prolly get in trouble. You know how Dad likes her." Marcello smirked as he said this and my stomach climbed into its pitted knot. I held my legs tighter to my chest, the fury wrapped up in fear and held tight.

"When's Dad coming home, anyway?" Kara whined.

"He went with my mom to Chicago," I blurted, and let go my knees.

"Again?" Marcello complained. "Isn't he Linda's boss? What does he need to go with her all the time for?"

"Pussy," Kara said, turning her gaze to me.

She glared at me as though it were my fault. Now that I'd released my legs, I got an idea. "We could play hide and seek." I continued, "Only we could make it the whole block, instead of just the house. It'd make it more interesting." I sat up and walked on my knees out of the corner.

I wanted to get Neil back. I wanted to get Kara back. I wanted them to know what it was like to not have a place, to not have clothes or a bed. I was happy with my idea. I could rush back to the house and lock them all out and leave them out there all night. I looked around at each of them. I saw mischief pass over Neil's eyes again. "Let's play the way where you find people though instead of jumping out at each other," I added.

Marcello shrugged and stood up from the couch. "Okay."

Neil's grin broadened and he got up. Kara glared at them for a moment longer before she finally got up to join in. "Fine," she said. "Let's go."

I couldn't believe they agreed. Because it was such a big area, you had to count to 1000. Neil was "it" first. Base was the house. My plan was going to work, as long as I could get a good hiding place.

As soon as he started counting, I took off running. My feet flew over the greening grasses and the first dandelions of the season. I picked a spot just on the wrong side of a tree trunk that would be easy to find but also easy to run back to the house from. I was too excited and couldn't think of anything better other than my fort and that was too far *and* I didn't really want anyone to know about it.

Before I knew it, I heard, "Ready or not, here I come!"

I was paralyzed and didn't run, like I'd planned, back to the house.

Instead, I heard Kara yelling "no fair" as Neil caught her.

I took off by it was already too late. Marcello had already beat me back to the house.

Kara was "it" now and we started over. The sun set quickly and the light played tricks on me. I tripped over a toy in a yard but continued on looking for a good hiding spot. I went to the end of the block thinking it would take her a while to make it over that way. I scoured the dimming light high and low. There was an aluminum encasement by the sunken windows of a two-story house. A possibility, but scary, because I might get stuck and then have to have some stranger pull me out of there. Nah.

I finally settled on a giant outdoor Tupperware toy box. I dumped most of the toys into a nearby tool shed and crawled in. Even though moments before I'd wanted to get revenge, lock them all out, now I was afraid again. And the fear made me just want to hide away safely. Before long, I fell asleep. No one found me.

I woke up the next morning to twin toddler screams.

"Mmommyyyy!!!!! There's a girl in my toy box!!!!"

"Oh shoot, shhhh." I held my finger to my lips and plead, "Sorry, I uh, fell asleep," I said groggy. Then I got up and started to run off, limping from my left foot falling asleep.

"Hey wait, you stop!" yelled the mom. But I was on the run.

Sunday dragged by uneventfully. No one said anything when I got back to the house. They didn't seem to have noticed that I'd disappeared from the game. They hadn't called police or anything. It was kind of messed up, but at least I knew I'd be okay when I got my bus ticket. It'd be a long time, if ever, before they called me in and that was comforting. My plan would work fine.

I wanted to get away from the Crosbys' for good. I was dying to go home and be with my mom. I couldn't stop thinking about how she had a plan and how she'd take us away somewhere and all our problems would be over. She'd take care of me. We'd live somewhere new and she'd have a car and we'd have a new place and no party friends or runs to Chicago. We'd have pizza and ice cream and play cards and she'd say goodnight to me and kiss my forehead.

Sunday night I agonized over when to leave. Would it be better to leave Monday or Tuesday? If I went Monday and they weren't back yet, I risked being home for a long time or not able to get into the apartment, or my mom and Dante staying at the apartment and not being able to talk to my mom and having to explain why I'd come and how I'd gotten there. But if I waited until Tuesday, I risked Dante coming back to the house and another night with him. That was terrifying.

Finally, I decided I couldn't risk another night with Dante. I'd go earlier. I'd always managed to figure out a way to survive at home by myself and could do it again now if I needed to. I was optimistic that my mom would be there and that if she wasn't, I could figure a way in to wait until she came back.

I could hardly sleep that night. I tossed and turned and questioned whether I'd made the right choice about when to leave. I thought of all kinds of things that could go wrong. I'd be about to drift off only to jerk awake worrying that I'd gotten the wrong information about the fare and wouldn't have exact change and wouldn't be able to board the bus. I worried a bus driver in the county might not pick me up without a parent. Or worse, if a cop saw me and asked about my parents letting me take the bus. I considered forging a note from my mother to allow me to travel alone. But I abandoned that idea. I'd gotten caught last time I'd tried to forge something from my mom.

It was just a dumb permission slip. As if my mom cared where I went on a school field trip. But she sure cared about getting called in for a meeting to talk about it.

"God damnit, Seffra. I got better things to do than go to that school of yours. You best be on good behavior from here on out."

As a result, I hadn't gotten to go on that field trip which was to a dumb science museum I didn't want to go to anyway. But they'd also gone out to lunch. For free. You got to eat as much pizza as you wanted. I pretended not to care, but my stomach growled for months whenever someone talked about science.

$$\mathcal{D}$$

When morning finally came, I was tired and a little slap happy from the lack of sleep and nerves. But I was determined to go. I pictured my mom hugging me as soon as I walked in. I pictured how she'd say she was just fixin' to come and get me. My mom would protect me and take care of me and it would all be better when I found her. I just had to go find her.

I dressed and shoved my stuff into my backpack. I took some clothes out to make room for the Ramen I hadn't eaten yet, just in case. Then I headed out the door.

The morning was crisp but the day held the promise of warmth as the sun snuck up low and clear over the horizon. When the bus pulled up right on time at five after seven, I stepped up and handed the driver exact fare and asked for two transfers. He grunted and I made my way back and took a seat in the middle by the window. The vinyl squeaked as I settled down. I rubbed a finger along a tear in the seat and the yellowing foam that poked through.

I watched the glittering office parks with their crisp green landscaping, telling me nothing was out of the ordinary all the way to 170, the inner belt, where the buildings grew closer together, tighter, less orderly. I transferred bus lines and things got busier, more normal.

Now there were people on cracked sidewalks. A woman with tight jeans and a huge bubble butt jutted her hips out as she walked, hurrying her toddler with a tap to the back of the head. A few young men in all red muddled about in a patch of grass. They each had a bandana tied around a different body part: one around his calf below the knee, one around his forehead with a triangle toward his left eye. An Eastern European-looking woman with her hair in a scarf carried three plastic grocery bags in each hand. I settled into the familiarity.

Muscles I didn't know had clenched slackened and my eyelids grew heavy. I'd be home soon and my mom would be able to protect me from all this.

I pictured my mom. My mom, my mom, my mom: her hair her lip gloss and her smile…

I heard a siren and snapped awake, afraid I'd missed my last transfer. My whole body retightened as I worried that I'd missed it. Then I worried about seeing my mom, and I worried about not seeing my mom. My stomach tightened and I felt sharp gas pains. I tightened against them and held it together. The bus driver assured me that it was coming up soon; I hadn't missed it, and she'd let me know when it was time to change. I relaxed a bit.

I switched to the red line, which stopped all along Grand Avenue. From there it was close to a mile to our apartment, but it meant a shorter ride on the bus and a shorter time to wait at the transfer station. So that was the route I took to get home.

It had been four and a half weeks since I'd been home. It felt like forever. I was suddenly too scared to see my mom. I just knew she'd be home. I felt panicked. She would be angry with me for coming home. She would be angry because she'd be hung over and exhausted from Chicago. Worse, Dante could be there. I couldn't bring myself to go home. I rationalized that I would go home, but I'd wait until around eleven or so when she was likely to wake more pleasantly, with less of a hangover. I wandered into Tower Grove Park.

I was sulking on the swings, thinking what to do, when I caught sight of a guy on a milk crate. It couldn't be…it was Boogie!

It's amazing how a familiar face can cheer you up when you're down.

"What are you doing here?" I asked.

"Well hello there, young miss! How's the Lord in your life today?" he asked

"The Lord seems to have stepped out for the moment," I answered.

"Hmmm. That's a predicament, needs some firmament." He might have been drunk, or just crazy. Never can tell. "I can make you a nice trade today, Miss Thang. I'll give you some words from the Lord, and you can tell me a new joke. How's bout that?"

"Yeah, okay," I answered thinking of a good joke.

"Oh I got one. Three guys walk into a bar. The fourth one ducks." I laughed a little.

He looked at my quizzically. I demonstrated. "Three guys walk into a bar, bam, bam, bam" I said, gesturing to show how they'd hit the bar. "The fourth one ducks." I ducked a little and missed the pantomimed bar.

"Oh, I get it," he said, nodding. "Not your best, though."

"I guess I'm not really *on* today…" I trailed off.

Then he stood getting ready to give me 'the good news.'

"Seffra, the Lord heals!

"He take His big ole' hands out and put 'em on where it hurt most and heals!

"He don't make no deals!

"He don't take out no dice, and roll em on ice,

"It's your soul He *heals!*

"What He use you may ask? Well it ain't so big a task as ya'll'd think, you know. He use the good news.

"Some other bums, they drink they rums, and don't get no good news, instead they bury they heads in *booze.*

"But not ole Boogie,

"he shimmy and shoogy,

"cuz Jesus ain't just words for me, no sir.

"Them other bums, who drink they rum, they all aslur, but boogey, he clear-headed. So you listen up.

"Ready?

"Jesus *dreams*. He *redeems!*" By now he was screeching and jiggling his hips as he repeated "Jesus *redeems.*" Over and over again.

And for some reason, the sight of his hips wriggling and his screeching struck me and I laughed. I laughed so hard I almost peed.

I laughed and laughed until a tear caught in the outside corner of my eye. I wiped at it and said genuinely, "Thanks, Boogie." And I headed off with a spring in my step and my spirits high.

⤢

I went home. I walked into the entryway, which had never been locked anyway, and then my stomach sank when I saw a white page taped to the door: "Notice of Eviction." Had my mom moved out? The door-frame was still busted. The wood splintered next to the lock. The wood was weak and rotted, the splinters showing the porous age of the wood underneath layers of dark green paint. Unsure what else to do, I managed to jimmy the door to the apartment.

I stepped in, and, closing the door behind me, walked slowly from room to room. The floor squeaked and I jumped. The levity and confidence I'd gained from Boogie evaporated. *Idiot. You should know where to step by now.*

Most everything in the living room had been cleaned out. The big furniture was out, but odds and ends littered the floor.

Where had my mom been living? It was clear she wasn't living here, but if not here, then where?

I surveyed the remains of our old apartment. A t-shirt here, a balled up towel there, all junk though. They'd probably come through soon to throw it all out.

But not today. Today, I figured it was as good a place as any, so I lay on the living room floor balling up my mother's comforter with the pink roses underneath me. I pressed my face into the blanket. Hoping desperately for the smell of my mother's perfume, I cried myself to sleep.

It was hours and hours before I woke up. I hadn't relaxed fully and really slept since I'd gotten to the suburbs; I was always on alert. Awake after such a deep sleep, I sat up, drowsy and for the thousandth time that day, thought what to do. I had *no* idea where my mom was, how to reach her, anything. My options were limited. I considered going to Mr. Jackson or Mr. Miller; teachers might be able to help with this kind of thing. But I wasn't sure if school was out for the day or maybe already for the summer. I thought of the social worker and my stomach knotted deeper. Suddenly I had to use the bathroom.

I sweated on the toilet wondering whether there might be whiskey left under the sink. I checked and there wasn't. On the floor next to the sink cabinet laid a discarded lidless container of my mother's lip-gloss. I stared sadly at it. I ached for my mother. A few dusty hairs clung to the sticky white plastic roller. There it lay, left behind and forgotten. Once a tool integral in making my mother beautiful, no longer useful, it laid collecting dust and grime. I clung to the idea of my mother's lips. I needed her help so badly. I needed her to charge in and do what needed to be done no matter who told her not to, even with a gun to her face.

My mother would never allow a man to touch me the way Dante had tried to. I remembered the way her breath smelled in the night when she told me to never, ever let a man touch me. I wanted to run the roller over my lips and smell the sweet, sweet strawberry.

I picked it up off the floor and held it to my nose. I closed my eyes, desperate for the scent. My eyes snapped open as a jolt of hope travelled through me. My mom never, *ever* left without lip gloss on. This was obviously not her only container. Which meant she was somewhere with the rest of her makeup. Maybe she really was in jail like Kara had said. The thought made me sad. I dismissed it. My mom was too smart and charming for that. Kara'd been messing with me.

Maybe they were still in Chicago. Or maybe she was at Dante's. That would make sense. They'd come back together and she'd want to see me so they'd go there. Or they weren't back yet. But even then, they'd be coming to the house now that there was no apartment to go to. Maybe my mom'd found somewhere for us to go by now but hadn't gotten to tell me yet. She must've let the apartment go because she was coming to the Crosby's for me. She always kept us together. I shouldn't have doubted her.

I had enough money to get back to the suburbs and the sun hadn't completely set yet, which meant I hadn't missed the last bus back. The Crosbys probably wouldn't even have noticed I was gone anyway. I could go back and find my mom. We could still be together. She could still protect me.

I splashed water on my face. Refreshed, I grabbed my bag and left. This time, I wasn't nervous about the bus trip at all. But I should have been.

11

When I got back, no one said anything about where I was all day. It was well after dark and Kara and her brothers were eating frozen potpies for dinner. There were two left they let me eat. I scarfed them down and then offered to help Kara with the dishes.

"Yeah, *now* you want to help," she said glaring at me. "Of course when there's *no* work to do, you offer to help." She added, "What a spoiled brat!" under her breath and stormed off to wash the dishes. "Don't even worry about it."

She was right. There were only plates. Everything else got thrown out and it wasn't her job to take the trash out.

I was curious if Dante and my mom had come back, but after the looks I'd gotten when I offered to help out after dinner, I didn't dare ask. I was hoping to watch TV with them. That way I could be quiet in the corner and they'd probably leave me alone. Plus, I could eavesdrop and hear if they mentioned their dad or my mom.

The hours dragged on. None of them said a word the whole time. They went to bed around eleven and so I finally pulled the couch out to go to bed in hopes there'd be news of my mom in the morning.

I felt like I'd just fallen asleep when I awoke to the smell of whiskey and the squeak of the sofa bed springs. Dante had come home. He was drunk. My eyes ached for moisture but I didn't dare blink. I stirred, lying on my side. I groaned, pretending to still be asleep, hoping he'd be discouraged and leave, and at the same time I was feeling around under my pillow. I found my Swiss army knife and curled my fingers around it. I felt the warmth of him near me. My back stiffened involuntarily and I rolled onto my stomach.

His hand grasped at the bottom of my nightgown. I had rolled onto my stomach in an attempt to protect myself from him but he was on me and it was impossible to move him. I was trapped beneath his massive weight.

The position had initially seemed like it would protect me from him. Lying on my back felt like an invitation, like my whole front was open to him all the way down. So instead of staying on my side or rolling on my back, I'd chosen my stomach. I really didn't want to be on my back, so vulnerable, like a flipped turtle on its shell. I thought he couldn't get me if I was on my stomach. But I was so wrong about that.

I clutched the knife under my pillow as the weight of him made it increasingly difficult to breathe. The pillow pressed against my cheek. The cheap fabric of the sheet was stiff and scratchy.

"Mmmm... girl you smell goooood."

"You're hurting me." I could barely get the words out.

My mind flitted rapidly from option to option, one after another in quick succession. I thought of escaping to throw up again, but he had me pinned and he wasn't listening. I thought of screaming but I didn't think I could even get a scream out and if I did, who would care? I thought about trying to fight without the knife but that seemed dumb. I had it in my fingers but I was pressed down so far I couldn't reach Dante to do any damage. Plus, I considered all the ways the knife option could go wrong. I could end up killing him, or maybe worse, I could end up *not* killing him. Then he might kill me. Any scenario I could think of was bad.

It was getting harder and harder to breathe and I began seeing twinkling stars in my vision. I was getting dizzy. I fought it and tried to breathe but I could only breathe shallowly and it wasn't enough. I got dizzier.

"Please, I can't breathe," I choked out.

How good it would be to lay and press my fingers into my eyes. I began drifting off to the thoughts of sparkling dark blue bursts...I even started seeing them.

His weight came off me suddenly and I took a desperate gulp of air. Spit hung from the corner of my mouth as I took another deep breath. He had my nightgown up around my waist now. He began tugging at my underwear. They tore and I felt his fat hands pushing so hard. I heard his belt clinking and the flapping noise of it as it slid out of the loops and felt his forearm holding strong across the small of my back. My body was stiff and I was angry and scared. I stiffened more but it didn't make a difference. I was trapped.

His finger pushed inside me and I felt like I had to pee. But then a warm rush came up me in an electric wave and it felt good.

It felt good.

What was wrong with me?

"You like that, don't you, you fucking whore? Just like your slutty mom." The pressure grew greater and I felt pain and fear and shame so big, bigger than the pain when I fractured my skull. I started to cry.

He slapped me. "Stop crying, bitch."

He rolled me over abruptly onto my back, into the exact position I didn't want, and my arm came out from under the pillow. I was suddenly so angry. Outrageously, overwhelmingly angry.

My hand sweat against the knife hilt; panic and rage burst from me. I reached as far around his barreled torso as I could with the knife and pushed the blade deeply into his back. Then, with a skillful swiftness I'm certain I didn't actually possess, I pulled it back out. I was still enraged. I stabbed him again, deeper this time. I pushed it so hard part of the handle sunk into his back, and it made a sort of *squelch* noise when it came out.

I could've sworn the movement came from someone faster and more practiced, someone larger and stronger. *Thank you, Uncle Phin. Thank you. Thank you.*

"My mom's *not* a slut!"

Shock flashed across Dante's face; the look was unforgettable. Absolute surprise passed over his eyes before he zeroed in on me. I saw the sheet on the sofa bed had come off the corner and electric blue sateen fibers shown through with shiny white flowers.

His look passed into anger and he chuckled, "I told you to remember who your friends are."

He gurgled through clenched teeth.

I narrowed my gaze and shook my head slightly. Why was he laughing? I just stabbed him. *Remember who your friends are?* What did that mean?

"What? Wha'dya mean?" I stammered.

"Your mom's in jail, you dumb brat. I was the only one your cunt mother could get to take you." He laughed again. "*She's not a slut.*" He said in a high-pitched mock-version of my voice, making a face. The whites of his eyes flashed in the moonlit room. I was terrified.

Then his look turned from smug to pained. He rolled off me, groaning now. I sat straight up and looked at him. The groaning stopped. I heard shallow breathing. I was afraid to go near him. I looked from him to the end table and back. Time slowed and I stared for another instant and a thousand thoughts came and went.

My mom was in jail. Dante went to Chicago by himself. That was why he had to keep going to Chicago now.

My mom wasn't coming to help me. She wasn't going to come fix it and take care of me. She didn't have a secret plan to save us. This *was* her plan. I saw the blue mattress sticking out and thought about putting the corner back on. It would get blood on it otherwise. I thought about Dante's crooked teeth when he laughed. I thought how I'd like to shove his fat fist into his fat mouth. I stared at the mattress, not moving. I looked back at the end table and gathered the courage to grab my clothes out of the drawer. Adrenaline was coursing through me. I needed to move.

"What's going on?" Kara walked in wearing a Care Bear's nightgown and rubbing her eyes. She flipped on a light and squinted.

I looked away while my eyes adjusted. I looked back. She had chipped hot pink nail polish on her fingers and two black rubber bracelets intertwined around each other on her wrist. When her fists fell and she got a look at her dad she jerked to attention.

"What the FUCK DID YOU DO?" She stared daggers at me.

My arm felt cold and far away with the knife held at my side, like it was someone else's hand.

"I didn't. I mean. It," I stammered, "isn't what it looks like. I was—"

"Daddy? Daddy, are you okay?" She began shaking him.

"I'll be fine," he said.

"What happened, Daddy?"

"I'm fine," he gurgled.

"I'll call 911. Don't worry, Daddy," she whined, suddenly sounding so young and small.

"You can't call the police, girl." He sat up and his face turned white. "You know better than that; think what all we've got here. They could, uuuhhh," he groaned, "bring the K-9. This'll be okay." He held his arms tightly around himself.

She rushed over to him and put a hand on his back to steady him. He huffed and breathed and some color returned to his cheeks but he was still pale. I'd been steadily inching my way closer to the doorway but I kept my eyes on Dante and Kara the whole time.

"Shouldn't we get you to the hospital? I could wake Marcello up to take you," her voice rose at the end in a whining, desperate plea.

He shook his head, gathered his energy and said, "We'll figure it out." His color started to fade again and he trailed off, "Just… need to… rest"

He fell back in a pile and his breathing was loud and labored.

My hand grew heavier with the knife. I saw blood on Kara's hands.

Kara wiped tears away from her eyes and left streaks of his blood across her cheeks. His pants were still undone and you could see his brand new boxers gleamingly white, drawing attention to what he'd just done to me. I took another step.

"Get out of here, now." Kara's voice was demanding again, big. She dropped her voice to a growl, "Get out."

I needed to run. I looked at the end table, the drawer was open and I could see my clothes.

"What're you staring at, *whore*? Get the FUCK out of OUR HOUSE! It wasn't enough when your mom basically killed my mom? You needed to stab my dad too?"

She was starting to cry now, real tears, like I'd never really seen her cry.

"My mom didn't do anything! Your mom died in an accident! "

"Yeah, an 'accident.'" She wiped the tears away, refueled by my words now. "Your mom was supposed to drive that night but she got too drunk, as usual. So *my* mom had to die. If your whore mother had been driving, my mom would've been fine in the back seat. And now look what you did to my dad!" she wiped her face and pointed.

"I didn't. I don't...You don't understand what he did..." I felt the need to get out. I couldn't explain. I just needed out. I looked at the end table again. I wanted my own clothes but I wanted out more. I took another step.

"Here," she yelled, throwing my clothes at me. "Now get out! You and your whole family, stay away from us! You're evil, toxic people!"

I caught the clothes and scrunched them into a bundle and tucked them under my arm and headed out the door. I took off at a sprint without the slightest idea where I was going. It felt so good that I leaned into it and ran and ran. I pushed the whole night away and barely felt the run. Blacktop asphalt met white concrete and my feet pounded and slapped against it. There were pebbles and gravel in the drainage but I barely noticed.

I pressed on and ran harder and harder. I stopped seeing. There was only the slap of my feet and the glorious feeling of my heels hitting hard against the pavement.

After a bit, the slapping grew quieter and softer and there was no longer pavement beneath my feet but soft, loamy earth. My chest began burning and I stopped, finding myself at the creek's edge.

I looked at my surroundings. I was panting.

I took some deep breaths and tossed the knife into the creek. I wanted that knife away from me. I didn't want to think about what had happened.

There had been drought and the creek was a two-foot wide trickle of water lost in a six foot bank of mud. I stood in my bare feet on the wet leaves at the bank of the creek and thought what a stupid place it was to throw a knife. Someone would see it for sure. I didn't want to touch it though so I watched the water trickle.

I wondered if Kara might be behind me like in the suspense movies, or worse, Dante. I turned paranoid, suddenly convinced that one of them might have followed me and now was looming behind me about to attack. Neither of them were, though.

Fuck, fuck, fuck. Oh fuck. Oh fuck. What had I done? *Oh my god, what just happened?*

I looked down and saw the blood on my hands. I was still barefoot and in my pajamas. What had I done? I pulled the knife out of the creek and set it down. I rinsed more blood off my hands in the creek, watching the clouds of red billow and pink, then go clear. The water was slow and cold and flecks of leaves and creek-grime got stuck to my palms and my fingertips. I flicked my fingers off, then re-submerged them and tried again and again for a clean result. I kept pulling them out only to find one pebble stuck or two specks of leaf-fragment. I'd try again and again with the same results.

Finally, I furiously rubbed my hands against my nightgown but then I had blood on them again. I wet my hands a final time, this time not looking at the lack of a clean slate when I pulled them out.

I turned to looking at the soles of my feet. They were cut up, but not badly. They'd be sore later, but for now they were fine. I picked small rocks out of the cuts, and rinsed my feet in the creek.

I changed into my clothes. I strategically scrunched up my socks and then pulled open the mouth and pushed my foot in, stretching the sock over my foot as carefully as possible so as not to rub the cuts more than necessary, then put my shoes on. I folded up my night-gown as best as I could and put it in my backpack. It still had blood on it, but I might need it. I could throw it away later. I checked my watch. Barely 4:00 a.m.

I was disoriented and tired. The world would be waking up in the next few hours. I felt sick. I felt the pitted knot and wondered at how I'd gotten here. I thought of how I'd broken the stealing rule. If I hadn't done that this wouldn't have happened. This was my fault. I thought of Kara telling me to get out. I knew the look of revulsion in her face was pure recognition of who I was, of my core, of the pit.

I thought of all the things Kara knew about me. She'd been my best friend for a long time. She knew everything. She even knew about Neil and the manhole cover. That must've been why she'd believed it when he told her we'd had sex.

Maybe she was right and everything had been my fault. I had always known there was something unnamable and nasty about me. My mom'd called me a *jezebel* and an *evil twat* my whole life. And there'd always been that thing, that pit of true disgust that planted itself in my gut. There was something wrong with me. This *was* all my fault.

And my mom wasn't innocent either. She'd been partially responsible for the death of Kara's mother. I'd never known that. No wonder Kara hated me so much. I couldn't tell her what her dad did. She'd never believe me now.

I wondered if Kara would tell the police if she had a chance. I knew Dante wouldn't let her go to the police but what if he ended up in the hospital and she told anyway? I wondered what she'd tell. Which things she knew about me that she might use:

the times she and I had kissed or what she thought happened with Neil? She might even outright lie, especially if she thought it would help her dad.

My eyelids felt weighted. Barbells of guilt and shame pulled me toward the ground and I lay down and drifted. The sparkling blues were long gone. Instead my mind drifted to the spots I'd stared at in the kitchen of our apartment and I thought of the bullet my dad shot my mom with. I was just like him after all.

My thoughts grew scattered and one after another stuck to me like the flecks on my hands. The idea of going to jail occurred to me and I thought I could do better than my dad. I could get out of it. I tossed the knife away from me. I was like my father. I couldn't kill right either.

My thoughts drifted to the splintering drawing I'd done of the window crack. I thought of the bullet and envied its resolve, its straight path. Then a flash of Dante's gritted crooked teeth and his self-righteous anger at me and what I'd done jolted me alert. I looked around me for signs of him. Desperately my gaze flitted here and there, scanning for him. He was nowhere to be found.

Get it together, Seffra.

I thought of the knife. I needed to hide it.

I searched for it in the long, dried-out grass. I found it and thought what to do. I couldn't toss it away, someone might find it. I couldn't stash it under a bush for the same reason. Maybe I could bury it? No, the overturned dirt would give it away and they'd find it eventually.

What to do with it? I finally settled on moving apart some larger rocks in the creek, digging a hole underneath them, and putting it there. I dug deep so I'd have plenty of soil to cover it with afterwards and so that when heavy summer rains came, it wouldn't get washed downstream. I set the knife in the hole then covered it. I made indents in the surface for the rocks to settle on. Then, I used the rocks to pound the indents into beds for them to sit. I set the rocks strategically in place.

I hoped police wouldn't be able to find it. If Dante died, they'd need a murder weapon to tie me to the crime. At least, that's what they said on TV. But maybe he wouldn't die. The police wouldn't be involved unless he died.

I dusted myself off and checked my watch. 4:37 a.m. My mind traveled alone in a long cold line. I ran my fingers around the edges of the glass pendant around my neck. I needed my mom. Needed her like I never had before. She would know what to do.

She would have picked us up without a second thought and driven us far, far away from all this. She'd done it before when she defended us. She'd kept us together. But now when I tried to defend myself, it didn't work. She couldn't help me. My mind slowed and turned weary. Images drowned into one another and the heaviness pulled me down further and further from images, into concepts. Large boulders and small fingers, something without form that drowned out shape but was only size and weight and difficulty, like a black hole sopping up light. It told me I was too big, not big enough, too narrow, not wide enough and the concept weighted my mind.

Three minutes is a long time. Especially if you may have just killed a man at the ripe age of twelve. My mother was in jail. I was on my own. She couldn't keep us together. She couldn't help me. I was alone and had to figure out my next move alone. I had no friends and no family. I had no one. I was alone and heavy.

At 4:40 a.m. I knew the only thing I could do, the only choice I had left. I was evil and nasty and this was what needed to be done to people like me. I had leaves and grime stuck to me. I was ashamed and discarded. With absolute certainty, I knew I needed to die. It was so simple.

So simple it must be true. The truth, the inevitability, the resolution comforted and warmed me. It gave my mind a set of problems to tackle, a solution to put into place. I took a slow breath; I was righteous and calm. I had a plan.

12

I had to figure out how to kill myself.

I didn't think I could stomach cutting my wrists. Especially because that would mean using the same knife I'd used on Dante, and that idea made me physically ill. I was pretty sure there were pills and whiskey back at the Crosby crash pad, and that seemed like a good way to go. But the idea of braving going back to that house was overwhelming.

I took solace in remembering the way I'd felt when the whiskey had made it to my belly. The warmth and the numb. I wanted that.

So I swallowed my fears. I figured the worst things that could happen already had. I was wrong, of course. Many harder things were to come still but I didn't know that then. I was right not to fear the Crosbys though. At that moment, there wasn't much worse they'd do to me. And I knew I was going to die anyway. Plus, I knew I could be in and out of the window in a flash. With all the adrenaline and the urgency of the situation, I'd bet it would take me less than a minute total.

I steeled myself with this information and climbed in the bathroom window.

I quickly surveyed myself in the mirror. I looked tired and my hair needed a brushing. My clothes were clean, and despite my paranoia about my neck, I'd gotten all the blood off. I took my necklace off and rinsed it in the sink again anyway.

I checked the medicine cabinet. Just as I'd thought: half a dozen orange bottles with white childproof lids. I read the sides for warning labels. If it said, "may cause drowsiness" I took it. Under the sink, like at my house, there was a clear bottle with a black label filled with amber liquid. I took that too and hopped out the window.

I wasn't tired anymore. I was clear and purposeful. I knew where to go and how to get there. I could get away from the houses quickly by hopping down into the ravine by the creek. I could make it without being seen by any neighbors. I had less than a block to walk before I could get to the creek.

Once there, I could follow water to Creve Coeur Park, where I'd determined to do it. It was peaceful and the woods were thick. There was a bluff overlooking the lake and a trickling waterfall at the base. It was a lovely place to die.

The walk was long. The sun wasn't up yet when I started out and I was hiking a ravine filled with sticks that poked at me as I went. It was slow going especially because of my sore feet. But the pain felt right as I got to the lake.

I smelled the freshness of spring. It was a beautiful park. The giant natural lake sat still as stone reflecting the white flecks of stars in its smooth surface.

I'd been at the park once when my mom had this nice boyfriend for a while. He and a friend had taken us there on their Harleys. I'd hiked around and sat in the woods, smelling the earth on my palms and enjoying the quiet against the bright clean air. It was a quiet you don't hear in the city. A quiet interrupted by birds and scampering things in the leaves.

This time as I walked along the paved path back toward the waterfall, a giant plop of bird poop splatted two feet in front of me. I looked up and saw an owl looking me right in the eye. I wondered if Uncle Phin had anything to do with his appearance. For a moment, as that owl looked me in the eye, I felt the wisdom of ages denounce my plans. I felt it say, "Life is not quitting." But deep down I did not believe there was any life left for me to live. I believed this was a gift, a way to celebrate and mark my last moments with dignity and beauty. It reassured me to look into the eyes of that soundless flyer, a bird that moved in the world without any disturbance. I would leave this world as an owl, silently, painlessly, simply.

I hiked up a steep hillside onto the target-shooting course. Where the paved path ended, a dirt one began up a steep incline that led to the course. I'd stumbled upon bull's-eyes on my previous trip there. Luckily there was nothing in season or about to be in season at that point and it was a weekday so there was no one around. Plus, a scenario where a target shooter missed and caught a piece of me was not uninviting at this point. The decision lightened my heart. I felt peaceful and right and good, settled and correct in my resolve.

I found a tucked-away corner and quietly ate my last stolen candy bar as the sun rose. I took my time and savored each bite. I enjoyed the crunch of the cookie as it broke and let the chocolate around it melt and smoothly dissolve in a bath of saliva.

When I was finished, I took out the soda and the orange pill bottles. I poured some soda into the liquor bottle and opened the first container of pills. I shoved a fistful in my mouth, and took a swig off the bottle. The fizz of the soda foamed up in my mouth and I coughed and spit a couple of pills out. I reached out and grabbed them off the ground and swallowed them again, this time with dirt in my mouth.

Container after container of pills I swallowed like this: deliberately. Pill after pill. All of them. Then I lay back against the slope of the hillside in the damp underbrush and watched the sky lighten seamlessly from dark to blackest navy, then deeper blues, truer blues, and the cloudy pinks and yellows came in with all those other unnamable colors that artists and God alone call familiar. I thought about how my drawings sucked anyway and should be thrown out. I was no artist; artists could paint beauty in colors that put their soul to a page. They could make you ache. I reached my hand out for them, begged them to become part of my repertoire of senses. I set my jaw against the grit in my teeth. I held the piece of glass around my neck to my lips. The drugs set to work and I slackened, loosened, and my jaw gave way to the earth.

The top of my head grew fuzzy, fizzly, and my belly warmer and warmer. My fears were far away now, my worries and flitting thoughts set down like wet butterfly wings to dry. I released into it and the concept came again. It was a blob of something simple, like a heavy black ink balloon, it weighed me down with sleep. I released and the ink balloon grew.

I pictured my mother; how badly I wished she could've helped me. Tears dripped and I jerked against my decision for a moment. But the concept was there.

I let go and the weight relaxed me. The ink balloon released its black. I leaned into my decision with dirt in my mouth. Or maybe it was sand. Or maybe something in between. Between night and day, between life and death, between dirt and rock, between sand and broken glass.

Part II:
Life Made Flat

1

If you cut into my skin, I'm certain you would find rings under the surface. Layers of concentric circles stacked against one another like a tree. Some subtle and fine, others dark circles, like life made thick and tired. Like a tree, I have evidence of the lives I've led. Instead of marrow, deep down I'd have sap, bleeding gently down my core from what happened when I was yanked from the life I had with my mom to this new life. From a life floating unguided in tumultuous waters, to a life pinned-down, controlled and determined as lightning to fix me fast. I hardened against it, fought it. Then flattened myself, learned, and made do.

Day came. The sunlight cut through the trees and revealed my plan. I became part of another plan, part of the trees then.

"Hey. How you feelin'?" A quiet woman's voice floated in. The source of the voice was a short, espresso-colored woman with shiny white teeth. I didn't internalize what she said, just stared and stared at all that contrast.

She shook her head and started to walk away. I wanted her to stay. "My head h- hu-" I attempted. Then, clearing my phlegmy throat, "My throat's sore too."

"Well, that's not surprising, now. They had to put a tube down your throat to pump your stomach." She spoke quietly.

The information slowly registered. I was alive. I was alive. Wait, why was I alive? Then, I didn't want to know. I utterly abandoned myself to the situation. I lay back in the abyss; I was no longer in control. I turned over on my side, found the fetal position and quietly cried.

"There, there. Things are okay now. You're safe and we'll find out how to help you. You rest." Then she rubbed my back in a couple of short, brisk circles and stopped.

"I'll make sure folks leave you alone for a bit so's you can get some rest."

I hardly acknowledged what she was saying. Just twisted myself up in tubes and pulled my IV-stabbed arms tighter around myself. I was utterly defeated, limp. My tears drizzled like long rain that will last as long as it lasts, soaking through lost shoes, making already discarded items even more worthless. Discarded.

I woke up to a doctor in the room. She had flawless skin slightly darker than cream. She wore a slight, carefully-applied coating of mascara and dark pink lipstick. She looked orderly and smart, professional.

She scooted up to the bed on a round black leather stool.

"I'm Dr. Lee. How're you feeling?" she said, clicking a pen and looking down at a chart.

I looked at her. The question wasn't worth answering. Tears welled up.

She waited a moment then asked, "What's your name?"

"Seffra Morgan," I answered automatically. I snapped stiff like someone had waved smelling salts under my nose. *They didn't know who I was. Why didn't I lie?* I slapped my hand over my mouth. *Why didn't I think this through? They didn't know who I was. Why was I so stupid?*

"Well, Seffra, I'd like to check your heart, and listen to your lungs. Would that be okay with you?"

I nodded. I didn't care.

I flinched when the cold metal made contact with my chest and belly, startled at feeling anything so sharp.

In the woods, I'd felt neutral. I'd floated away, a fuzzy non-entity. But cold, sterile instruments have a way of snatching you back down to earth. I sat forward, and she pulled my gown to the side and pressed the cold metal to my back.

"Seffra, you were very lucky those teenagers found you in the woods," she began. "Do you remember?" I must've looked puzzled.

I shook my head.

"You took a lot of pills and you likely would have died if they hadn't found you when they did. I don't want to scare you but I want you to understand that this is serious. You got here in time and we pumped the poisons out of your stomach. We're going to need to keep you here for a couple of days though to make sure your organs weren't damaged. Your liver especially can be seriously damaged by acetaminophen."

Then she said, "Seffra, are you safe? Is there someone trying to hurt you?"

The tears that had stalked my cheeks took their leave and dripped down. "I don't know," I answered, near-hyperventilating. "I mean, yeah. Of course. You know..." I trailed off, lying, knowing I shouldn't have said anything.

"Okay, take a deep breath. You're safe here. But we're going to need some information from you, alright? There's a policewoman outside the door who'd like to talk to you. She's very nice and you can take as long as you need talking to her. You don't have to tell her everything today either. She can come back if it gets too hard." She raised her finely tweezed eyebrows, tilting her chin down and looking at me, waiting.

A policewoman? I was terrified. What if they found out what I'd done? The hyperventilating grew stronger and I hacked and jerked.

"OK, breathe. Deep breaths. Just breathe."

It had been a tremendous help to the medical personnel to have all the bottles because they knew what I'd taken in order to treat me. But from the police perspective, the bottles were confusing.

They'd come from all sorts of places. There was Vicodin with one name on the bottle and Valium with a different one and Xanax with still another name. The police had the names on the pill bottles as leads that might help them figure who I was, but they hadn't followed them yet since there were all different names and so they suspected the pills had been either purchased illegally or stolen. The police needed to proceed with the utmost caution given my minor status and the uncertainty of what crimes might be involved.

I didn't know anything about the pills I'd taken, where they came from, what they'd do, but I figured they were prescriptions and if I took enough of them, it'd work. I'd die. It hadn't occurred to me that some teenagers messing around before school might find me.

In the afternoons, the park filled up with teenagers. The lower level of the park had a 15-mile-per-hour strip with parking spots alongside it. At the end of the strip was a loop with a waterfall. The large lake lay alongside the strip and sparkled especially brightly in the spring sun.

Teenagers came out there to cruise around in freshly washed and waxed sports cars, raised-up trucks, and recovered Impalas. They did a loop, parked and listened to music, stood around with friends and then did it again. But that was in the afternoon and even then they seemed to stay in the loop, not veering further back to the trails. I hadn't thought they'd go snooping down a trail near dawn. Plus, I was off the trail a little ways. So it was pretty miraculous that anyone had found me.

The police officer interviewed me carefully. She didn't know yet that I'd killed a man. I didn't know yet that I'd killed a man. I thought Dante might recover. I was interviewed as a *victim* then.

I left my hospital bed and walked with my IV bag in tow on its metal tower, down the slick, echoing hallway to a hospital social worker's tiny office. I sat across the desk from the officer, cramped in the barely ventilated room.

The officer talked with me about how it would work, what she would ask. Then she set up a video camera in the corner above her and pushed a button. A red light flashed.

"Please state your name and age for the record."

"Seffra Morgan, twelve."

"Seffra, do you know the difference between a truth and a lie?"

Do you? I should've asked.

Instead I answered questions and more questions. She asked questions about where I'd lived before and who lived in my house. She asked what I liked to do and where I liked to hang out. She asked where I went to school and what I ate.

I relaxed into it. I answered the easy questions and bragged about all the things I knew how to cook but how it was good to store up on food at school. Then I got so comfortable that I told her how I came to live with the Crosbys. Before I knew it, I was telling her about going to Chicago on runs.

Once I'd opened my mouth, I went on and on. I told her about how I took the bus into the city all by myself.

"It took almost an hour to get back into the city, but I watched for my stops and did the transfers I was supposed to and got there anyway." I smiled. "But when I got there, my mom wasn't there and our stuff was gone too." My smile evaporated and I stopped talking.

"Why did you decide to go find your mom?"

I remembered myself. I heard my mother: *Don't say a word to the law.* I shrugged and stared down, my lips tightly closed. *Idiot-girl.* The cop tried a different angle. What had I done, telling the police all this?

"So when you got to your old apartment and found out your mom had moved, what did you do then?"

I killed a man then ran. I didn't say anything though. I panicked. I shook and heaved.

"Okay. It's okay." She clicked the tape off. "Really, it's okay. We'll try again tomorrow."

I promised myself to shut up next time. I didn't want to go to juvie.

It was really late by the time I was done with the police officer and the nurse came in. The beautiful, gentle nurse from earlier in evening was gone and the night nurse was on now. She was a tall, stick of a woman, and abrupt.

"Seffra?"

"Yeah."

"The policewoman said you were hungry."

"Yes ma'am."

"Well, unfortunately you won't be able to eat anything for at least twenty four hours. Some of the medication you poisoned yourself with contained Acetaminophen."

I gave her a confused look.

"Acetaminophen is what is in Tylenol. In large doses it can destroy your liver. Your stomach was all pumped out. But because of the large amount that you took and your age, we're going to need you to drink some things to avoid permanent damage."

This new nurse was scaring me. *Permanent damage?* My eyes grew large with fear.

Unsympathetic, she shoved a cup filled with a watery black substance toward me.

"It's activated charcoal. It will absorb any poisons left in your stomach in order to prevent liver damage. Drink it."

I made a face looking into the cup.

She shook her head and *tsked.* "It tastes nasty, but that's what happens when you try to kill yourself by taking a bunch of pills. You'll need to drink a glass like this every four hours for the next twenty four hours."

The activated charcoal made me think of the dirt I had in my mouth swallowing the pills. It made me think of my soul and of Dante and what I'd done. What I deserved.

I looked out the window. Where earlier it had been bright and sunny and I'd seen leaves outside dance their way to the ground, now it was dark. It was deep dark, filled with sludge and time that doesn't move. Evening had fallen and I fell with it.

"Thanks," I said, taking a sip. I coughed and gagged a little and looked up at her.

She stood, immovable, waiting. She would make sure I took the whole thing. I drank it. Without a word she took the cup, turned on her heel, and left, making a note on her clipboard as she went.

She woke me throughout the night to drink the vile black liquid that tasted exactly like what it was called. Activated charcoal tastes like simultaneously drinking a glass of water and chewing on a barbeque grill. It's a bad night's remaining ashes, blackness, falling and falling. It's nasty.

That night in the hospital I had Technicolor dreams. They were grey and black with iridescent accents: turquoise and orange. I dreamt that I was scrubbing, scrubbing my body with large rocks. I was standing in a river but it had turned perpendicular to the ground and the water kept pouring harder and harder on me. The water turned from an aqua to charcoal gray, and then loosed itself into the orange of my mother's hair. It was a torrent of hair snaring me and then suddenly it released.

Water again, the pressure slowed to a trickle. I looked down and the rock I was using had turned to a brick of charcoal and while I wanted to, I could not stop rubbing charcoal into the cuts on my feet. Then I saw myself. I had dimples of gathered black in all my pores and my skin was dark. When I tried to look at my face, I saw

Mr. Miller, my classroom teacher, and looked at him. He was saying, "Seffra, terrible argument. What kind of idiot comes up with that drivel? I guess I overestimated you."

I was so angry, but when I went to punch him, my punches were like an infant's. I felt myself lose all power from within. There was absolutely no fight in my blows, no power to my resolution. And, desperate to get the power back, I looked up. Instead of my own reflection in the mirror, I saw the espresso-colored nurse. I looked for her gentle smile but instead her teeth tumbled out one after another. She stood, teeth tumbling from her face, cackling at me.

I woke up drenched in sweat and screaming with a nurse standing over me.

I had scratched the IV out of my arm and was still screaming and scratching at my arms. There were bright red wet spots on sheets where the IV and my blood had mixed and splashed. The light of the room and the bright red contrast to the white sheet, it was the same as the color contrast from my dreams. I scrambled up and sat holding my knees to my chest, panting.

The nurse shushed me and said it would be okay. She sat on the bed and hugged and rocked me for a few moments until my breathing started to go back to a regular pattern.

"You had a bad dream. Lots of folks do in the hospital. Take some deep breaths."

She re-attached my IV. "I'm going to give you something to help you sleep," she said and brushed my hair back from my face exactly the way a mother would. "Someone will put fresh sheets on for you soon," she said and left.

Fresh sheets and my hair brushed and the heavenly rush of cool calm that came from the drugs in my IV. Who could ask for anything but an eternity of the same?

Morning always came though. In the morning I saw a social worker. She asked me some of the same questions as the police officer plus a whole lot more. She wanted to know more about what had happened, more about my mom. She asked me about my depression and how I felt now. *My depression?*

"How much do you drink? How often do you take drugs?" She sat, her legs crossed, in a chair on the side of my bed with a notepad where she periodically took notes.

I raised an eyebrow in irritation. I blurted, "I don't…" *usually.*

She wanted to know if I was still suicidal; I wasn't really sure. All I knew was that I wanted her to stop talking to me.

"Can we be done now?" I asked and looked up at the IV, imagining that cool rush, hoping for it.

"Soon," she said. "Seffra, now I have a difficult question to ask. When you were found, the medical staff went through your things for clues about who you were, what may have happened, what you might have taken. They found some helpful things in there." A long pause.

I remembered my nightgown and knew immediately this was what the buildup was all about. The turquoise from my dream was the same as the flowers on my pajamas.

"Seffra, they found a nightgown with some blood on it. Can you tell me about that?" Her voice was so calming, you could almost pretend the questions she asked were normal. It was lulling. She was relaxed with her hands folded on top of her notebook, waiting.

I shook my head. Harder and harder, I shook until it wasn't just my head but my whole body shaking and I began to heave just as I had with the police officer. And there were turquoise flowers and cinnamon bursts of light.

"You have all the time in the world. I'm gonna need to know about that nightgown though, about the blood. Take your time."

I shook my head more but the flowers and lights were long gone. There were only white sheets and a steel bedframe and pasty green walls.

"It's okay. I can wait." A slight nod, and more calm, her wrists limp and relaxed against the white page.

I snorted and blew my nose. I took a deep breath and looked up. I wasn't sure what I should say. I couldn't lie, but I was afraid to tell them what had happened. It seemed likely that they wouldn't believe me. I would probably spend the rest of my life in jail, just like my father, and now my mother too, for what I'd done. After all, the Crosby kids certainly wouldn't back up my story. And I had no idea if they'd talk to Kara and what she'd say. Whether she'd tell them about seeing her father's pants down or if she'd tell them I was a whore and I'd touched her. I had no idea.

But I also had no idea how to lie my way out of this. My mom would have known how to lie her way out of it. I tugged the sheets around me; the bloodstain from the day before should have been stiff and dry now. I searched for it, but through the medicine they had come and changed the sheets. I wished for the grit of the dried blood in the old sheets to hold onto, to set my jaw against. I had to lie.

"I cut myself climbing a fence." I searched looking up and to the left, then saying, "Sleep walking." My knuckles were getting sore from holding on so tight.

"Uh huh." She nodded and waited a moment before uncrossing and crossing her legs. "Seffra, you can tell me what happened, you know. The truth. It will take some time, but we're going to find out. It'll be better if *you* tell me. Then I'll know better how to help you."

I wasn't sure where to start. Every time I thought about telling her anything, I started to get sick and have trouble breathing. I put the pillow over my head.

"Whose blood is on the nightgown? Is it yours?"

"No." Then through sobs I said, "It's Dante's."

I pulled the pillow off.

She was looking at me and her gaze was soft, I could feel it. Her pity was almost more than I could bear. She asked in that soothing voice, "How did his blood get there?"

"You won't believe me. I know it." I sobbed harder.

"Just tell the truth about what happened and people will believe you."

"But I...I mean, the things that I did and he—" I choked. "He... tried to..."

At this point I started to panic. I stopped talking and started hyperventilating again. "And, and..."

I could not breathe well enough to go on. People wouldn't believe me. Why would people believe me?

I wanted my dream back, the pressure of the water dumping on me and the scraping of the rocks against my skin shaving away the past. I wanted a shower. I needed a shower.

"Seffra, it's okay. Take your time," she said and waited. "You don't have to tell me everything at once."

"Please, I—" I stammered, then through sniffles said, "I need a shower—please." *Please.* I whined and begged.

"It's okay. I can wait."

Again she waited and after a few minutes when I didn't say anything, she finally said, "Did he hurt you? Or try to?"

I nodded but part of me knew I was discarded and not to be believed. I'd been left behind with no more thought than my mom's lip gloss on the bathroom floor of our old apartment. Part of me knew that dirt and muck stick to discarded things and that no one would put much stock in what I said. I was a thief who'd gotten drunk in the woods after trying to kill a man. Now all I could hope for was freaking out badly enough that they'd give me more drugs and I could float away into an ever-lengthening night.

"I'm going to need you to tell me about it. But you don't have to do it right now. And you don't have to do it with words. You can write it down, or you can draw a picture. But for now, why don't you work on getting better, okay?" She put a hand on the edge of the bed, patted it as she stood to go.

Then, "You're safe now, and we'll figure out how to help you. You can trust us."

My fingers ached from clenching the sheets so tightly. I pulled the covers up and curled my arms underneath, releasing my hands. I was exhausted from the conversation and ached for my mother. I needed her to hold me and hold me the way she did when I fractured my skull. I wanted her soothing voice calling me "baby." I wanted to smell her perfume while she caressed my forehead and told me everything would be ok. But she was in jail and it would be a long time before I got to see her again.

I slept some more and woke when I was supposed to and drank their nasty drinks. I showered at least two or three times a day for an hour or longer. I let the water pour on me and wished I could make it harder, hotter. My skin turned pink and itched. I wished the water could blast my skin right off. I longed for food, but I understood what a terrible thing I'd done to myself. The stick-nurse's eyes told me how unforgivable what I'd done was and she didn't know the half of it. So the emptiness in my stomach felt right. I set my jaw into the justice of it.

2

I saw the social worker more times after that including one time with the police. During the police interview, officers came and they videotaped the conversation again. We met in a conference room at a large table with new burgundy-upholstered office chairs. I'd just gotten out of the shower and my hair hung wet. I felt good, clean. I swung my feet; the scrubs they'd given me too long hung over my feet. I stared at the blinking red light.

Again I had to agree to tell the truth. And I meant to. I did. But there were things I couldn't speak. There was truth in what I didn't say. Plus there was what Kara had to say.

"Where were you when Dante came in from the bar that night?"

I gestured with my hands next to my face to show that I'd been sleeping.

In a monotone voice, the officer spoke into the recorder, "Let the record reflect, the subject put two hands to her face to indicate sleeping."

Then more gently to me: "Can you draw the room where this took place?"

I drew the room including all the furniture. We talked about what each thing was and what had gone on. When I got to the sofa bed I drew red hatch marks all over it and a blob of red in the middle. I looked up, nodded slightly, *do you see?*

They got from my drawing that I'd been attacked.

"How many times?"

I held up two fingers.

"How did his blood get on your nightgown?"

I thought I was telling them. I thought this was the truth. I thought they could tell. I thought a lot of things. The police officer seemed so nice. She seemed like she believed me.

I gestured and gagged to show how I'd thrown up. Then I said, "In the bathroom."

I'd started to be confused about what happened when. I didn't know when I'd thrown up and when I'd stabbed Dante and when he'd touched me and how far it all had gone.

"Who else knows about this?"

I wasn't really sure if Kara knew. I didn't know if she'd tell the truth about it if she did know. And I really couldn't keep it all straight. And when I tried to, I got so sleepy. I literally couldn't keep my eyes open. And I thought I'd told them all of it. So I drifted off.

The next time I saw the social worker it was without the police. I was back in my room and the lights were dimmed. I lay in my bed, more comfortable this time. I fiddled with the IV while she told me why she was there. Her purpose was different this time. It wasn't just to find out what had happened with Dante and that night, but to figure out the situation in my home over all and come up with a plan for me. Until this meeting, a plan had not occurred to me. Anything beyond the moment and being in the hospital hadn't occurred to me.

"We don't know where your mom is, Seffra. We're doing everything we can to find her."

"What do you mean? I thought she was in jail. She's not?"

She paused then and continued carefully, "She was. But she bonded out and we're not certain where she went after that. Even when we find her, I need you to know that we can't send you home with her. At least not for a while."

"What? Why?" I said, immediately tearing up. I fantasized about nothing more than my mother's comforting hugs and now they were saying even though she wasn't in jail, I still couldn't have any.

"Well Seffra, your mom…" she stopped, choosing her words carefully. "Your mom didn't keep you safe. We can't send you back to her unless we're sure she will this time."

"But it's not her fault! It was mine, I mean, she didn't *do* anything wrong. I'm the bad one. Punish *me*. She didn't *do* anything."

She got a serious look on her face and leaned close. "Seffra, I want you to listen to me very carefully. You didn't do anything wrong. Nothing you did makes it okay for your mom to leave you the way she did. Nothing you did makes it okay for Dante to have done what he did. This is not your fault." She spoke each word carefully and searched my eyes for recognition.

I nodded, but knew she was wrong. I was disgusting. Dante Crosby's touch had felt good and while I tried to bury that deep down, it was still there. When Neil Crosby had said nasty things to me back in our old neighborhood, I'd liked his attention. I'd played dirty with Kara Crosby and kissed her even though she was another girl and my friend. Something was wrong with me. Something dirty and nasty, so dirty and nasty it didn't have a name. This was my fault, my doing.

Plans were made for me by case workers, doctors, and therapists. They decided I would go to a treatment center after leaving the hospital. My sleep had been disturbed by horrific nightmares and I woke up screaming often. They strapped my arms down at night to try to keep me from pulling out my IV but it only made things worse. The reasons were obvious and the medical staff got a scolding for how this could be traumatizing me all over again. So they stopped doing that and gave me medication to help me sleep. It made me groggy but I stopped pulling my IV out and got better.

Medically I was stable now. I wasn't suicidal anymore and my liver function was fine thanks to the activated charcoal. I could go to a home if I had one. But the team thought with the level of trauma that I'd experienced and how much difficulty I was having talking about it, plus the trouble sleeping that I wasn't a good candidate for a foster home yet; I'd need treatment first. That and when they asked me where I wanted to go, I told them to fuck themselves if they thought I'd go to any foster home. I wanted my mom, not some crappy stand-in in frumpy clothes.

3

It was a Saturday at the end of May when Alison, my newly-assigned case worker, pulled up to the curb of the hospital in a dirty white Honda Civic. It was a sunny, cloudless day. The kind of day where the whole world should chuck their plans and lay in the grass.

The seatbelt automatically whirred back into position when I shut the door. I glanced up at it.

"Oh that?" She flipped her hand. "Don't forget to fasten the lap belt."

Huh? This bitch had better be joking. Two seatbelts? My mom never made me wear *one*.

Alison got in and the same thing happened with hers. She fed the lap belt from her left to her right hand, clicked it into place, turned to me and smiled.

"What do you like to listen to? I've got DJ Jazzy Jeff and the Fresh Prince "summertime," or some Nirvana or…" She rolled the window down and I did the same.

"Summertime," I said and clicked my own seatbelt into place. Alison was growing on me. The tape she popped in turned out to be a mixtape and she sang off-key at the top of her lungs to a whole variety of top 40 songs as she drove too fast around the turnstile entering highway 270. We drove on with the wind tunneling noisily through the car and her singing for another 20 minutes before getting off the highway.

She turned the knob and the radio volume fell, then clicked off.

"So what questions do you have?"

I shrugged, caught off-guard, not knowing what to ask.

"Ok, well, I can tell you some stuff anyway and you can ask me questions as you think of them, 'k?"

She was chipper, blonde, pretty and young. I was warming more than I wanted to.

"You're going to Castlerock, which is an RTC." She must've noticed my confusion because she continued, "Oh yeah, RTC is short for residential treatment center. It just means you'll live there. Anyway, it's an RTC for kids 7-17. You'll be living in the girl's cottage."

"Cottage?"

"Yeah. That's what they call the houses where the kids live. You'll see." She changed lanes and we slowed down as she turned the blinker on to turn..

"What about the other kids? What are they there for?" I cracked the knuckles of my middle fingers.

While she talked, we sat at a red light and Alison reached back and grabbed her purse from behind my seat. She rifled through it, located a wallet, pulled it out, then replaced it and zipped her purse back up.

The light changed and she continued, "Well, there are lots of kids and they have different reasons for being there. They may have behavior problems, or they may be there while their parents are working on trying to get them back home again. But then some kids' parental rights have been terminated. All the kids need a place to figure things out. So yeah, there's a variety of kids, basically."

I wondered about the *parental rights have been terminated* but part of me didn't want to know.

She undid her seatbelt and opened the door. "I think you'll like it. It's a bunch of kids who are struggling with their situations just like you. You guys'll be able to help each other out and get better."

There was a little truth in that, but mostly it was a far more brutal social structure.

I did learn a lot from my situation and from being at Castlerock, and I did make friends and find people who wanted to do better, but it was far from this idyllic communal healing center she described.

I picked at my clothes and heard my mom telling me *sit still*. I dropped my hands into my lap and chewed in the inside of my cheek. I had no idea what to expect a treatment center to be. I didn't have much time to worry about it though because then she pulled into the parking lot of a discount clothing store.

"First things first. We've got to get you some clothes," she said and pulled the brake up firmly. We rolled up our windows and stepped onto the asphalt.

I only had two outfits in my bag, neither of which really fit well anyway, when I left the Crosby crash pad, and the pajamas with the blood on them had been taken for evidence. I was twelve and starting to get boobs. I needed training bras, but my mom had never bothered. The discount store had nicer stuff than most of the clothes I'd owned. Most of my clothes came pre-stained from the thrift store. These clothes were stain resistant and I could even pick them out myself. At first I ran my hands over things but didn't pick anything out. I didn't know what I could spend or what I was allowed to get and I didn't want to sound greedy by asking. So I just stood there. Meanwhile Alison started grabbing things and piling them on my arms. When she realized I was standing there holding a giant pile of clothes, not moving, she sent me to the dressing room to start trying things on.

She called me out to check the fit of the clothes and helped me pick out what worked best. She told me I was darling, said the new clothes looked fantastic, and congratulated herself on her ability to spot a sale. She bought me a bunch of new things: a skirt, several new tops, two pairs of jeans, socks, underwear, two pairs of pajama pants and tops. (I would never again wear a night gown.) I got an entire wardrobe basically in one day.

The shopping trip helped me loosen up and we chatted the rest of the way to Castlerock.

"Castlerock's in St. Peters, which is a little ways from the city. There's a park close by the kids walk to all the time, and you'll have your own room." She glanced over not moving her hands from ten and two on the steering wheel.

I was listening and nodding along, taking it all in, watching the scenery go by, when she said, "There'll be fun activities all summer, not just school."

I raised my eyebrows. "School? I'm sorry, what?" I turned and looked at her from my seat.

Oh fuck this. I could skip school and look for my mom. School, seriously?

She chattered along, not taking her eyes off the road, not acknowledging my tone. "Many of the clients—"

"Clients?"

"—yeah, sorry, kids. The kids have academic problems and are behind in school, so they have to go year 'round. Plus, with all the treatment during the year, it helps to stay caught up academically if they go year 'round."

I was annoyed but she didn't seem to notice. I blew hair out of my face and looked out the window.

She told me there were tons of staff members who'd help me with any problems I had, and that I could also always call her if I had any problems.

"And you'll tell me when you find my mom, right?"

She nodded. "Of course. But Seffra, I don't want you to worry too much about your mom. Concentrate on getting everything you can out of treatment. These people are trained professionals and they want to help you. Focus on that."

She could tell I wasn't giving up that easily so she added, "It could be a long time before we find her. There's really no way to know."

4

Castlerock was a complex with multiple buildings nestled in neat and trim landscaping: sculptured round hedges, retaining walls with hollyhock and butterfly weed. The main building loomed in the center of the complex. It was a mustard-colored brick building that housed the school and a bunch of offices and meeting rooms.

From there were pathways to other smaller bungalows they called cottages. Alison pointed out the different buildings as we went to the cottage I would live in. There were kids everywhere with helmets and bikes and scooters and basketballs. It looked like a commercial for children's health care or an ad for an after school program.

"How come they're all boys?" I asked.

"That's a boys' cottage." She pointed to her right, then pointing to her left, "That's the girls'."

It just so happened that when we arrived, one of the boys' cottages were out playing. There were two cottages divided by a large grassy area and swings and a jungle gym. She assured me there would be girls for me to play with in my own cottage: a girl's cottage.

I overheard someone asking "Who's the new girl?" and felt like everyone there could see me, like everyone there knew everything about me. It was one of the most nerve-wracking moments of my life.

I thought I'd have toilet paper stuck to my foot or boogers coming out of my nose or something and everyone would know but me.

"This is Waterfalls," she said as the door to the house opened, "where you'll be staying while you're here."

"Waterfalls?" I said raising my eyebrows in disdain. *Really? We weren't going to have to hold hands and sing Kumbaya and shit, were we?*

She ignored my attitude and said, "Waterfalls is a safe place for girls ages 7-17 who are at-risk."

I wondered *at risk of what?* but not enough to ask.

The walls were painted in pastels and there were pretty framed pictures on the walls of the girls who lived there. There was a bulletin board that said "Waterfalls: Girls of Promise."

Puke.

The door opened into the kitchen, which had a dishwasher and small table in it. The kitchen opened into a great big living room in the middle of the cottage. There were padded wooden one-person chairs situated in a *U*-shape around the TV. There was a teacher's desk off to the side and a teenaged-looking boy and girl talking quickly back and forth next to it.

"Can I come out now?" came a call from a doorway. Small fingers curled around the doorjamb and an arm disappeared around the corner.

"Not yet; we're still doing quiet time," the girl said.

Turns out both the teenaged-looking people were actually working there. The guy added, "We'll go out to rec in a minute."

Huh?

Just then the guy looked up and said, "Oh you must be Seffra! We're so glad you made it!" He sounded like a Mouseketeer, he was *that* enthusiastic. But he was kinda cute so I let it slide. "We're just about to go out to rec, would you like to come?"

"What does *that* mean?" I asked.

"It means—" he drew a breath, "—we're going outside to play for a while."

"I don't know, maybe I should put my stuff away first. Maybe spend some time in my room…"

I learned quickly that when staff asked you a question, they were really telling you what you had to do. I also learned that room time was not something you could just do whenever you wanted. My life was about to change drastically.

After years of doing things when I wanted—eating when I wanted, sleeping when I wanted, coming and going when I wanted, years of being left pretty much to my own devices—someone else would now decide all of these things. To go to your room you had to wait in your doorway and say, "Can I go back now?" Same with when you wanted to leave your room. Then you had to ask, "Can I come out now?"

Staff put the food on the table and we all had to sit in silence for fifteen seconds while some kids prayed and we'd wait for them to say, "You can start," before trying to be the first to grab the good stuff and shovel it all in. There was a whole lingo to this place and it would take a little bit to figure it all out.

There were seven other girls in the cottage with me. They were keenly interested in who I was because I was new. Every time a new kid moved in, it changed the social structure a little and the adjustment made everybody anxious. Like a pack that has to reorganize and figure out where the new dog belongs in the pecking order, bitches get nervous.

The girls had already done 'deep clean' that day so we had the rest of the day for 'rec' and activities. We were having pizza for dinner, which was delivered by the food service people on a cart. We heated it up in the oven, but they delivered the prepped food.

The kitchen was nice, although impersonal. It was neat and large with counters free from dust, grime, and all manner of decoration. It had beige self-adhesive-style countertops, and pine cupboards stained light. The stove was a simple black stove, frequently used and immediately cleaned.

It was not a professional kitchen but there were signs of insti-
tutionalization even there. A card hanging against the backsplash
next to the stove saying when the oven had last been cleaned. A
sign hung on the door between the garage and the kitchen alerting
workers to "contact your supervisor if injured on the job and be sure
to fill out an incident report within twenty-four hours." Also, a large
laminated poster on the wall of the laundry room with big capital
letters: "OSHA Worker's Rights." I liked how clean and orderly it was
and that I could tell that chores were shared. I also liked the clean,
disinfectant smell.

The food was good. I had seconds, then thirds until I thought I
would burst. You could eat as much as you wanted as long as everyone
else had gotten a chance to eat some too. I was stuffed when we had
room time again. It was the first chance I had to unpack and settle in
with my belongings.

I removed the tags and carefully folded and put away my new
clothes in the drawers. Then I looked out my window. I could see one
of the other 'cottages' across the courtyard and curiously watched
from the window for a while. No one stirred at the boy's cottage
across the way though. I was gathering my courage to ask if they had
a book I could borrow when I heard a commotion in the main room.

"Nnnnooo!" a little girl's screechy voice came.

"Sabrina, it's not time to come out of your room yet. I'd appreciate it if you would go back in your room please," came the guy-
Mouseketeer's calm voice.

"Nnnnnooo! Fuck you!" she screamed, flopping to the ground
and kicking her feet wildly at the guy.

"I'm gonna take a step back now, count to ten, and expect you to
find your own way back to your room."

"Fuck fuck fuck fuck fuck," she repeated over and over, mixing in
a cackling giggle. She found a rhythm and it became a kind of song.
"Fuck fuckity fuck fuck, fuck fuck fuck."

The guy did what he'd said he'd do, but the girl moved closer.
"You guys, we've got it under control; I'd appreciate it if you would go

back in your rooms." Several kids shuffled back into their rooms. I stayed in my doorway, eyes wide. Just before they grabbed her, Sabrina made eye contact with me.

"This is your last warning. Either you're going to start calming down or you know what'll happen." His voice rose on the last note.

Her eyes met mine and she got a slight grin and hocked a *huge* loogie right at the guy. Both adults moved swiftly, and in one coordinated movement grabbed her, took her to the ground, and flipped her on her stomach. The girl Mouseketeer was toward the top half of her, the guy toward the bottom.

I couldn't believe my eyes. They were holding that little girl down and she was screaming and cussing, saying the most vile things you ever heard at the top of her lungs. It was like watching *The Exorcist.*

"Get your bitch-ass hands off me!" She twisted and writhed and screamed, "You'll go to hell for this, you mother bitches. You skinny fucks." Then she spit and slammed her head against the hard, vinyl floor, smiled and did it again.

I'd stepped out of my room and walked toward them without noticing what I was doing. I now stood over them wide-eyed.

"Seffra, get back in your room!" came a barked order. I quickly did as I was told.

A girl from the room next to mine said, "you'll get used to her." And that made it all even crazier. You got *used* to this?

As I crossed the threshold into my own room, she added, "Sabrina's parents fractured her skull in like three places when she was a baby."

"Whoa, what happened to her parents?"

"Mostly nothing." I could hear her feet moving around and then she appeared in my doorway. "Their rights got terminated, but they didn't go to jail or nothin'."

"How do you know all this?"

She rolled her eyes and leaned against the wall as she slumped back to her own room, "I'm going home tomorrow. I don't care if you believe me or not, new girl."

I reached my head as far out as I could, trying to see in this girl's room without leaving mine. "I didn't say I didn't believe you. I just wondered."

"It's small here. Everybody knows everything. You'll see."

Sabrina's restraint continued and I anxiously listened to what was going on. Sabrina swore and spit and yelled for help. I was too scared to do anything but listen, though. What *was* this place? Why me? I mean, I got in fights sometimes, but not like that girl. She was *crazy*.

Time crept on while my mind raced and my ears strained for signs of what might be happening. The outbursts of spitting and cussing grew farther and farther apart when I heard the guy say, "Sabrina, I'm going to let go of one hand. I want you to leave it where it is." He said this in an even, calm voice. I could hear her panting and sniffling, but nothing happened. For a moment, it was quiet.

"Ok, you're doing great. I'm going to let go of your feet now." This time it was the girl.

Long, quiet pause. More heavy breathing.

"Ok, I'm letting go of your other hand and moving to the wall. I'd appreciate it if you'd sit up."

I heard shuffling then just sniffling and it was quiet for quite a while.

"Would you like some water?" came the girl's gentle voice.

More quiet, waiting.

"Here you go."

Sabrina went to her room and took a long nap. And I sat on top of my bed, not wanting to touch anything, wishing I were back in a pay-by-the-week hotel in Chicago waiting for my mom to come back from the bars.

I vowed to get out of there as fast as I could and get back to my mom where I could pretend none of this had ever happened. I thought of Uncle Phin and wondered if he could help hurry me back home.

Uncle Phin, I really need you to help find my mom so I can get out of this crazy place. Please help me get home.

5

Monday came and Uncle Phin hadn't delivered anything on my mom. So that was my first day of school, even though it was supposed to be the start of summer.

School at Castlerock was nothing like regular school. We had almost no homework ever. Unlike my old school where no one bothered to do it, at this school, the teachers didn't even bother to give it. Instead we had treatment work, which consisted of doing worksheets about feelings and how to be a good friend and why we started fires or touched ourselves or threw things or cussed; there were lots and lots of cuss sheets.

School started and ended at normal school times and we mostly had the regular subjects, but there were so many small differences, you couldn't mistake it. It'd be like if all of a sudden all the doorknobs were on the wrong side and light switches flipped the wrong way and clocks followed time counterclockwise. Enough of those little things add up. You feel almost dizzy or feverish with a kind of culture shock you can't escape.

Our teachers were not like the teachers in public school. They joked around with each other a lot more, were animated, and wore t-shirts and jeans almost every day. And while they still thought school was important, they seemed less consumed by their subjects.

They seemed to recognize that there were other things going on in our lives. Or maybe they were just bad teachers. Who knows.

We traveled from class to class with our cottage, which I figured out right away meant there was no way the classes could teach all of us. There were kids in our cottage who couldn't read. At all. Like, not even "cat." Then there were other kids who knew algebra and read at a college level.

The first morning, I panicked over not having any school supplies. I asked around the cottage about it, but no one seemed to think it was a big deal.

"The teachers'll make sure you have what you need for your classes," was all they'd say.

"But I don't even have a pencil!" I emphasized. "How am I going to do math or write in a journal without a pencil?"

I didn't worry as much after the first week though. No one brought pencils, or paper, or books. We kept almost everything for each class in the classroom and didn't bring much with us between times. After I saw some of the crazy shit that went down at Castlerock, I figured kids would've stabbed each other in the hallways if they had pencils with them and maybe that was why they didn't have us take stuff from class to class.

There was one boy, Danny, who had three things he had to bring to every class: his teddy, a cracked container of Silly Putty, and a basketball-shaped eraser. If he was missing any of those things, he flipped shit. I mean, flipped. Shit.

One day, he left the eraser at the cottage and kept sucking his fingertips. A new counselor who'd just started that day gently asked him to take his fingers out of his mouth. He pointed at the full eraser at the end of his pencil. "But, I just need my ewaseh (eraser) so badwy." He baby-talk answered as if this should explain it.

When she pointed out that that *was* an eraser, he punched her in the face and was restrained three separate times before someone finally took him back to the cottage to get the damned basketball eraser. He literally skipped around for the rest of the day kissing the eraser, smiling and hugging it to himself.

Some of the kids just needed their stuff a certain way like that. They needed their notebooks organized and to wait until the end of writing an essay in order to put every period in and dot every i. Other kids never knew where anything was and would lose the previous day's most prized belonging without a care.

There was a girl whose caseworker had given her a photo album filled with snapshots of her sisters who had been adopted out. In the mean time, this girl was set to age-out. Aging-out is what happens to kids who don't find homes by the time they're teenagers and so they finish out their youth in facilities and never have a permanent place.

She carried the album around for days showing snapshots of her sisters to everyone who would give her the time: her darling sisters with matching bows in their hair sitting on grassy lawns drinking lemonade. She was so cheerful about the whole thing. I thought it was weird. I mean, why wasn't she pissed off her sisters weren't with her? But none of us really noticed when she stopped carrying it everywhere.

We didn't realize she'd lost the album until staff returned it after cleaning out her cubby for her. When they did, she simply shrugged and shoved it back in the cupboard, slamming the door and walking away.

We had a homeroom where we met each morning for breakfast and check in. We filed in and set any personal belongings like jackets (in winter) or purses in our cubbies and then sat at our desks for check in. Check in was when we said what'd happened to us the night before and our goal for the day. We had behavior sheets they called logs, which followed us throughout the day. We wrote our goals on our logs. We picked things like, "stay on green," "no cuss sheets," "have good boundaries." After making something up to put on our logs, we handed them in to one of the two staff members who worked in the classroom.

That was another thing at Castlerock: there were adults *everywhere*. They never left us alone in a classroom, not even for a second. They never left us alone in our cottages, except at night and even then they did bed checks all night every fifteen minutes. They waited for us outside the bathrooms and listened in on most of our conversations. There were specific people designated to work in the hallways just waiting to deal with kids who got kicked out of class or left even though they probably just wanted to be alone. We were never left alone. It was maddening.

$$\mathfrak{L}$$

On the first day, we shuffled into the classroom.

An olive-skinned man with gelled hair clapped his hands and jumped down from the table he was sitting on.

"Welcome!" he said really loudly, yet somehow was not yelling. "You must be Seffra. I'm Horatio," he said and put his hand out to shake mine.

I knit my brow, unsure what to do. But he suffered no such uncertainty. He grabbed my hand and shook it vigorously. My arm felt jiggly and warm.

"So glad to have you with us."

He seemed to mean it, too. Was this guy serious? "Don't I need a pencil, and, I don't know, some paper?" I asked.

He whooped and said, "This girl's got *questions*. That's great, Seffra! No, not yet. Teachers in your classes will have all the supplies you need. What else you got, girl?"

"Aren't *you* my teacher?"

He laughed loudly. "Me? Noooo." He drew out the no, making it several syllables long. "I'm your treatment counselor."

"Treatment counselor? Why do I have a counselor in my classroom?"

The other kids snickered.

"Well, because this is treatment, Seffra," he said and then, "You'll get it. Just give it a couple days."

I shrugged and stopped asking questions.

There was a huge schedule posted on the wall on red butcher paper. We had breakfast and check in first thing, then Math, then Science, then Reading, then Group, then lunch, then Social Studies, then Specials (PE, Library, Art) then homeroom/checkout, then back to the cottages.

At the end of the day I found myself drooped over my desk back in homeroom for checkout.

"So, how was it?" Horatio asked.

I lay my head in my folded up arms and didn't say anything. I hadn't even realized he was talking to me.

"Seffra!"

"Huh, me?" I snapped to.

He looked from side to side dramatically. "Anyone else here named Seffra?" He searched under papers. "Pretty sure you're the only one. You might be the only one in the whole United States!" He smiled broadly, revealing straight white teeth. The corners of his eyes were deeply lined from smiling and sun.

My eyes were big now. I just wanted to go home and take a nap. "Fine, I guess," I slumped further.

He punched some numbers into a calculator and abruptly shouted, "Look at *that*: 98%! Seffra, you're starting off strong."

I shrugged and he came over and dug his hand into my shoulder blades in a massage that was too hard for me. I jerked at his touch but reminded myself I was fine and didn't complain because he just seemed too excited about it all, I didn't want to disappoint him. He moved on.

The kid next to me elbowed me and whispered, "That means you're on green tonight."

Each day the staff would tally up the total during checkout. There were points you could earn for being on task, for being polite and helpful to peers or staff or both, for cleaning up after your-self. Then there were points you could lose for about a million dif-ferent things. You could lose points for swearing, for disrespectful language, for 'aggression,' for 'failing to follow directives,' for 'poor boundaries.' If you had a 90% or higher average each day that de-termined your 'level' for the evening. You could be on green, yel-low, or red. Green meant you could watch TV and eat sweets, and the staff was generally nice to you. Yellow or Red meant you had to deal with questions and comments about your school behavior all evening and you didn't get to do anything you asked for without a comment about "I don't know, you're not on green." It also usually meant extra treatment work, aka worksheets.

The Mouseketeers from the weekend showed up to take us back to the cottage even though it wasn't even a block away and didn't in-volve crossing any streets or anything. We still couldn't walk that far by ourselves. Like I said, there were adults everywhere.

"I'll take the logs," the guy said and gathered them up and we walked back.

"How was your first day?" the girl Mouseketeer asked.

I shrugged. "I'm tired and I just want to go to my room."

I stared longingly toward my doorframe. The doors had all been removed from the bedrooms for safety. The design prevented you from seeing into a person's room directly since the entryways were almost like in nice hotels with a hallway area and beds set back and to the side of that mini-vestibule, but it was still a distinc-tive difference. Each room held a pine-framed bunk bed beyond the empty doorjamb and tucked back so that you had some privacy. The furniture was all nearly the same but the comforters atop the beds were different.

I slept on the top bunk because I felt like I could see someone coming easier that way. It made me feel safer, like I could pop up, jump down and take off at a sprint if I needed to. I'd never had a bunk bed before (or a room without a door.) It was difficult to make the bed but otherwise comfortable. I liked being high up and pretended at first to be away at camp.

But today I was so tired, the idea of walking back and climbing up the ladder and pushing back the lavender comforter seemed an insurmountable challenge.

I placed my hands on either side of the doorway. "Can I go back now?"

"Yes."

I collapsed on the bottom bunk, even though there were no sheets, and fell asleep.

Room time that day was far too short. Seemingly moments after falling asleep, I was awoken.

"Treatment time!" A Mouseketeer.

I slumped into my padded chair in the *U*-shaped living room where I was handed three ring binder full of "treatment work." For an hour we had treatment time which was working on "feelings worksheets" out of our binders. The staff read our logs for the day from the school and we set goals again for the evening. Then our evening routine began with the night's chores or taking showers or whatever and then dinner, TV, and bed. I was exhausted at bedtime and slunk to my bed. This time I didn't give in to the exhaustion but climbed the ladder and nestled under the comforter.

I lay in the dim light. Without a door, and with staff in the living room, there was light that poured in. I'd have thought that would be annoying, but I found it comforting to know that there was someone outside the door. I knew that no one would be coming in my bedroom at night. No one.

That led me to Dante. I pushed that away but then thought of Kara. I wondered what she would do to me. I thought of the way she'd overturned my desk and taken my drawing notebook. I thought of the look on her face after I stabbed her dad. I knew if she saw me again, she'd seek revenge. I didn't know what she'd do exactly but it would be bad.

The window was a small square with beige mini blinds closed tight. No light filtered through. There were no bugs in the cottage either that I saw. The only sounds were staff shuffling papers around on the desk and whispering. I stared at the walls. They were smooth, without any cracks. I wondered what the walls were like in my mom's jail cell. I wondered if she thought of me and if she had a plan to get us out of this. I missed her like crazy then. I wanted to be home with her.

I thought of the cracks in my wall and my windows at home in our old apartment. I thought of the bullet hole that I'd always imagined, but there was no crack to give purchase to that thought. The footing just wasn't there.

I wasn't at home. I was at Waterfalls in treatment. I gave up thinking and fell asleep.

Staff woke me up the next morning to start it all over again.

6

The first week went by in a blur. Check in, check out, goals, logs, hygiene, room time, school, rec, and on like that.

On Friday morning, Horatio was his usual enthusiastic self. But on Fridays, things were a little different.

"Seffra! You've been on green all week. Fantastic! You get to go to Friday Fun this afternoon."

I was so exhausted by all the new terms, I couldn't even bother to get excited. "Okay," was all I said.

"Okay? *Okay?*" he shouted. "We're going to the zoo this afternoon. And all you have to say is okay?"

I looked down. I couldn't tell if I was in trouble or not. He clapped me on the back.

"We're going to have a fantastic time, Seffra. Okay?"

I smiled in spite of myself.

We went through our normal morning routine but around eleven picked up sack lunches and took them on vans to go into the city. Most of the kids were going but a few had to stay back, including Sabrina, the girl who I'd watched get held down by staff over the weekend and Danny, the boy who needed to bring three things with him everywhere. If you'd been restrained during the past week, you couldn't go. You had to "show that you knew how to control your body first."

It was pretty much just like at regular school when you went on a field trip except we took vans to get there and there were a lot more staff with us than chaperones at regular school. Which meant they were listening to everything we said.

When we arrived at the zoo, we picnicked by the sea lions. I stared gratefully out in the heat, not even caring that sweat dripped down my arms. The heat rose off the asphalt in wavy black lines that reminded me of how I felt when I was drunk at my house. The numbness, the not needing to say anything or do anything. It was just good to sit and not think and watch the sea lions diving in and out of the water and barking at each other. I ate my sandwich gratefully. Lunch was over before I knew it and staff hollered at us to get our stuff together to go.

This girl Brandy raised her hand and volunteered to collect trash. She went from table to table, smiling sexily at all the boys and jutting her hips around as she bent over too far to pick up the brown paper bags.

"How old is she?" I asked the girl next to me.

"Eleven, but she used to be a hooker. That's why she looks like that."

"No fucking way."

"Seffra!" Staff again.

"Sorry," I said. "It slipped."

We walked around the zoo as a group for a couple of hours. When we got to the big cats, they gave us some time to mill about, letting us know it was the last stop before returning to the vans to get back in time for dinner. By then, I was so hot I just wanted to get back to the air-conditioned school.

A lion with a full brown mane lounged in the shade, napping in the heat. It was too hot for even the savannah animals to be doing much. I turned my attention to Brandy, who was talking to a boy who had his back turned to me. She leaned into him with her dainty hand on his shoulder. She laughed a like a songbird and he handed something small to her. She palmed it and seamlessly stuck it in her pocket. I perked up. She turned my way and winked.

Wait, I knew him. He was a dealer from south city who hung around my block sometimes.

"Aw shit. That you, Seff?"

I just stared.

"I thought you'd be in juvie. Didn't you kill a guy?"

Brandy raised her eyebrows suddenly keenly interested in me.

"I, uh, I don't know what you're talking about," I answered, ducking down and trying to walk away.

"Yo, watch out for that girl," he warned Brandy. "She *killed* a motherfucker."

Had I? Jesus. I mean, I knew I could have killed him, but not that I *did* kill him.

Then he called after me, "Don't worry, girl. I won't tell Kara or those Crosby boys I saw you. I don't want trouble."

I bumped into Horatio. I'd started half running without even knowing I'd done it.

"Seffra?" He looked concerned but I couldn't see straight. I was dizzy. So dizzy. *I killed a man. I killed Dante.*

Then it all went black.

The next thing I knew, it was check out. I didn't even know what day it was.

"Can I see my log?" The log would give me information about what classes I'd had and how the day had gone. Maybe it would jog my memory.

"Seffra, this is not good. You're not going to be on green tonight. You can't get out of here with behavior like this."

The Mouseketeer handed me the white paper. Tuesday. It was Tuesday. I didn't even remember coming back from the zoo much less how it had gotten to be *Tuesday*.

I was confused and so, so angry. All I knew was that everyone was looking at me and I'd done something wrong. I didn't even remember what I'd done.

I looked at my log hoping for answers. It was filled with tally marks about boundaries, swearing, and notes about running. Running? I wasn't surprised that I'd been swearing but this looked really bad. I'd never gotten in this much trouble. I mean, I swore here and there and got in fights every once in a while, but that stuff was always a momentary thing. This was an entire day of running, swearing, and pushing. I didn't remember any of it. *What was going on?*

"I guess your honeymooning period must be ending."

I was suddenly uncontrollably furious at that Mouseketeer for her chipper voice, for listening to every word I said, for never leaving me alone. For everything. Fuck her, honeymooning period. Fuck her. I didn't even remember any of it. Fuck her and this whole place. I wanted out. I wanted destruction.

I looked her in the eye and lifted the paper. I tore it in half, slowly. Then ripped it in half again and again.

"Maybe you're just getting *your* period, ya fuckin' bitch!"

The stress of every decision made for me, of dealing with *crazy* kids, of being around chaos all the time, of not even remembering how it had gotten to be Tuesday in the first place had gotten to me. What had I done?

And the truth is, I'd just been attacked, and had just found out that I'd killed a man, and I was feeling it. No one could tell me about my mother and I was now in an institution. My life was no longer my own and I rebelled. I wanted out.

"That's two cuss sheets Seffra. If you're not careful, you're going to lose all your TV time." She reached her hand out to take back the log.

"*Oh no, am I gonna lose TV time?*" I mocked. "Like I give a flying fuck."

That made three but I didn't care. It felt so good to yell at these assholes. I'd gotten cuss sheets before and they sucked to do. Each cuss sheet meant you had to write out the definition of five new words from the dictionary. Then you had to use the words correctly in a sentence. It took hours because inevitably I'd get frustrated when I couldn't figure out which definition in the dictionary, couldn't figure out which was a verb and which was a noun and then I'd be frustrated and cuss again and then I'd have more cuss sheets. But this time, I didn't care what anyone was going to do to me. I couldn't hold it in anymore, not the swearing, not the fury at being controlled, not the frustration of being away and not knowing when my life might be my own and certainly not my language.

The spite I felt toward the staff fueled my unspoken promise to myself not to break down, not to give in to them. They couldn't make me do anything I didn't want to do and I would prove it.

"You can't tell me what to do; you're NOT MY FUCKING MOM!" I screamed and ran from the classroom.

7

Alison showed up at the end of June. Caseworkers were required to see their clients every month, so at the end of the month, you couldn't take three steps without bumping into somebody's caseworker. I'd been trying to call mine. I'd call and get her answering machine and leave a message. Then staff would tell me that she'd called back but it would always be when I wasn't there. By the time I finally saw Alison, I'd been at Castlerock for a little over three weeks and it hadn't exactly gone smoothly.

We sat at the picnic table just outside the cottage to talk. I stared at my hands and she asked, "So, how's it going?"

"Okay, I guess."

"Really? Because I hear you've been struggling: running, cussing…What's going on?"

I mumbled, "I don't know," and she stared sternly at me with her eyebrows raised. Suddenly, I blurted out, "Maybe because I'm a killer." My face flushed with shame at what I'd said. I pulled my feet up on the bench and held my knees and looked down. I stole a glance and saw her face move from stern to sad to confused.

"A killer? Why would you say that?" She held her purse tightly to her chest.

I looked up and released my knees. "I'm right, aren't I? Dante's dead, right? I killed him. Right?"

"Wait, someone told you about Dante? Who? How? No one should've talked to you without my okay."

I sneered.

She released her purse, setting it down on the bench. She got out a pen and notepad and then asked, "Okay, what did you hear?"

"Nothing. I don't know. Some guy from my neighborhood said I killed him. It's true though, huh?"

"How did you talk to someone from home? You're supposed to be in treatment here. Was this when you ran away?"

"*Ran away?* I never ran away. I left a classroom a coupla times, sure, but I didn't *run away*. Where would I go?" I got up and paced in front of the bench.

She breathed deeply and stared at me for a long time, not saying anything. Then she said, "I think we got off on the wrong foot. Seffra, I came to check in on you. It's my job to make sure you're safe. The main purpose of our visits is to check on safety and to help you be successful in treatment so you can get out and go to live with a family."

I sat back down. "What do you mean a family? I have a mom."

"I know that, Seffra. But your mom didn't keep you safe and we don't know if she'll be able to when you're ready to leave either. I hope so, but we just don't know."

I folded my arms and slumped down lower on the bench.

"I want to talk to you about Dante. Let's back up."

Pause.

"He did die. He died in the hospital two weeks ago. And it looks like you stabbed him, but I suspect you did it in self-defense. He didn't go to the hospital right away and the injury he sustained shouldn't have killed him. It didn't hit any major organs but he waited days to go in. You were very traumatized when you came to the hospital and we think it was because he hurt you. We think he hurt you and you defended yourself and then didn't want anyone to know about it so he didn't go to the hospital in time and died. The police are going to want to talk to you about it again. They're going to need to interview you."

"Because I killed him." I stared at my fingers.

I thought about what Kara would have said. I was intensely curious at the same time as shit-your-pants scared to know what she'd said. I pushed it down though, deciding that I didn't want to know. If they hadn't charged me yet, maybe she didn't say anything. Maybe she died too. Then I felt really shitty. Of course she hadn't died. And probably she hadn't told the police anything. Maybe she was going to leave me alone. Or maybe she was going to try to get me back herself. Or maybe she was a horrible distraught mess from her father dying. I felt terrible again. Because she was alone now just like I was. And I was responsible.

Alison made a face. "Self-defense is not the same as killing someone. The police have questions about the information you gave when you were in the hospital and they need to make sure they've done their due diligence. The police think you lied about where you stabbed him and so they're concerned that you may have lied about other things as well. They need to be thorough and they need to be sure."

I was pacing again. I alternated between pacing and then slamming my body down onto the bench and staring at my feet. I was so angry. And so sleepy. I didn't know how to be so angry and so tired at the same time. I sat back down and started to give in to exhaustion and cradled my head in my arms on the table.

"Seffra, it's not uncommon for victims not to remember everything when things like this happen, to be unclear about what happened. You just have to be honest. I'm on your side here."

She sounded like she was telling the truth, but somehow I knew I was on my own just the same. This was her job. But this was my life. I knew my mom was the only one who could really help. *Don't say a word to the law.*

I looked up. "I didn't lie. I'm not a liar." I kicked the ground below the bench and felt the friction of the rubber of the sole of my shoe against the concrete. I kicked it again, harder, and felt my foot warming.

"Okay, well, I believe you. I'm on your side," she said again. "You're going to have to talk to the police about what happened. I can be there. But you're going to have to answer some questions."

I was about to say fuck it and go inside and try to take a nap, but then I asked, "What about my mom?"

"That's the other reason I'm here," she said. "Your mom's in jail, serving a few days, but she'll be out soon. I'm going to see her after this."

I was all ears. Alison talked about what my mom would have to do to see me. She'd have to get out of jail and get a job and a place to live.

I was nodding along, thinking *she can do all that, easy* when she told me that my mom would have to be sober. At that, I leaned back over my arms and sobbed quietly. She'd never been sober. There was no way. I wasn't going to see my mom again. Ever.

I couldn't stop crying and could hardly hear what Alison was saying. My mom was the only one who could help me. But I just kept thinking how I'd never see my mom again. I wished I'd refused to drink the activated charcoal that had saved my life and my liver. Why did those teenagers have to go poking around where they didn't belong? I wished to be back in the woods, dying.

I barely heard Alison talking. She was far away, her voice at the end of a long spiraling tunnel. She went on about how long it would be and about how the first visits would be with a therapist to help my mom and I talk about everything that'd happened. She chattered excitedly as though it were all going to be rainbows and kittens.

But that kind of talk couldn't last forever. Sooner or later, reality always came calling.

When my visit with Alison was over, I went back to my new life in the cottage and slept through whatever they tried to make me do for the rest of the day.

8

Now that I knew (or thought I knew) that I wouldn't see my mom again, I lost all hope for my future for a while. While I kept up with routines, I did the bare minimum. I had neither the energy to rebel nor to put forth actual effort toward excelling. I floated along, and they kept up with all the treatment. I could hardly stand it. There were worksheets on trust, and on repairing relationships, and on truth and lies, and on who can touch your body, and when to call 911. They were endless.

I definitely couldn't stand the constant focus on *getting out of here.* Why should I try to get out? I had nowhere to go.

While sweeping: "Seffra, you know if you don't work hard on your deep clean, you'll get dropped to yellow and yellow doesn't help you get out of here."

In Science class: "If you guys can't get it together to do a simple experiment here, it's going to be really hard for you when you get out of here and into public school."

In group therapy: "You're going to need to know how to get along with other people if you're going to make it when you get out of here."

On field trips: "You guys can NOT act like this when you get out of here."

It's no wonder that by the time I sat down with my therapist, I didn't want to hear anything else about what I needed to do to *get out of here* or what things would be like once I *got out of here.* Frankly, I didn't want anything to do with therapy by then. All I wanted was to read books, watch TV, and eat junk food. I didn't give a crap about anything else.

So when I met with my individual therapist, Francie, I couldn't be bothered. I slumped into my seat and crossed my arms and stared.

"How's your adjustment to Castlerock been so far?" she asked, making small talk.

"Oh amazing," I said in a high-pitched, sickeningly-sweet voice. "I'm just loving it all. I'm such a girl of *promise*, you know." I rolled my eyes.

She set her notebook down in her lap, pulled her glasses off her head, and exhaled. But she didn't say anything. She gazed softly, blinking frequently. I stared at the second hand ticking around the clock on the wall while she said nothing.

I tapped my finger on my arm. "What?" I asked finally.

"Nothing. I'm just wondering what that word means to you."

"Huh? What word?" I asked over my left shoulder.

"Promise."

Oh puke, I thought, but I didn't say anything.

"We can talk about it another time though." She put her glasses back on and changed the subject. "I know Alison came and spoke to you about Dante dying. How are you feeling about that? That's heavy stuff." She had round glasses, giant dark circles that covered much of her face.

I unfolded my arms and sat forward a little. "I feel fine." I squinted. "Why wouldn't I? That guy tried to rape me. I'm fine. He's the one who did something wrong, not me."

"Tell me more about that."

I bounced my leg. "No. Isn't it enough that I have to tell the police about it? I didn't do anything. I just defended myself and now everyone's after *me* to explain it and talk about it and FEEL about it. I mean, what the fuck? I'm fine." I stood up. I was escalating quickly but didn't really want to do a cuss sheet so I sat back down and said, "I'm sorry. I shouldn't have cussed."

"That's okay. Seffra, in here, you can say whatever you need to. This is a safe place for you to talk about whatever you need to."

"Wait, I can cuss in here? Seriously?"

"If that's what you feel you need to say, then yes."

Whoa. I was paying attention now.

"Fuck," I said, cocking my head to the side and looking for her reaction.

She blinked.

I leaned forward. "Shit. Fuck. Shit. Bitch. Asshole."

Nothing. I sat back in the overstuffed chair. Huh?

"Bastard, mother-fucking shithole motherfucker assface!" I yelled.

Still nothing.

"FUCK," I screamed stretching it out until my voice was scratchy. Then I panted a little and smiled.

"Feel better?"

"Yeah, I do. I really do."

"Good," she said, her voice loud and clear. "It's hard to get through daily life when you're that angry. How does anger feel in your body?" she asked.

I had no idea. So then she asked, "Well, you feel better now, so how does *that* feel in your body?" She interrupted herself, "Actually, don't answer me. I want you to draw a picture of how it feels." She handed me some paper and some colored pencils.

I sat there staring at the paper while she said nothing. Finally, realizing she wasn't going to say anything else, I just started coloring. I didn't try to make shapes. I reached my hand up for where my necklace should be, the necklace I always wore that my mother gave me and then went back to coloring.

I made stairs and doors and windows. I made cracks in the doors and the sidewalks and I colored the deep reds and blues and blacks of those cracks. I felt lost in the page and the colors, so much so that I didn't notice the tears until there were several drops on the page.

I looked up. "It feels quiet when I'm not angry. It feels loose in my wrists and I feel still inside like water. And then I get sad." I was suddenly angry again. I tore the page in half. "This is stupid."

"As soon as you mentioned being sad, you tore your drawing up," she said.

"I hate being sad. I don't want to be sad." I dug my fingers into my palms.

"It seems almost like being sad makes you feel angry? Is that what's going on for you?' she asked.

What a stupid question. I reached for my necklace again and got angrier still. I just wanted to be with my mom again. I wanted my old life back and to go back to my bed and my notebook and have things be normal.

"Angry might feel more comfortable to you than sad."

I shrugged. "I just want to be done now. I miss my mom and I just want to see her. But I'm never going to see her again because of these asshole social workers!"

"Is that what makes you sad? You're worried that you won't see your mom again?"

I started crying and nodded, burying my face in my hands. "I just want my mom," I sobbed, choking and rocking.

"Well, I'll see what I can do about you seeing her then. I think it would be good for you as long as we can have a safe way to have you two visit."

I choked back a sob. "Really?"

I looked up and searched her face.

Francie nodded slowly. "Of course. Sure, Seffra." She nodded again and set her pad down. "I mean, she will have to be sober for a visit. But I want to get a visit going for you."

I rolled my eyes. "Damn," I muttered under my breath.

Francie looked at me gently for a moment then narrowed her eyes. "Remember this is a place you can say whatever you need to. Swearing is fine in here."

"You can't make my mom sober. Don't you get it? I tried for years to make my mom sober. I tried being good. I drew her pictures and cleaned the house. I was quiet and good when she told me to be but it never worked. Do you know how many times I dumped liquor down the sink and how many times she beat me for it? But I did it over and over again because I just wanted her to stay home and take care of me!"

"I'm sorry, Seffra. You're right. I can't make your mom sober any more than you could. No one can. Only your mom can make that decision."

"She promised. She'd promise to stay sober but she never did. Never." I could barely get a breath in now.

Francie put her hand on my back. "I'm sorry Seffra. I know you love your mom and miss her. I'm sorry she didn't keep her promise to you. I know it'll be hard but I hope we'll be able to get a visit for you and your mom."

I kept crying. I missed her so bad. I cried thinking of her perfume and how it felt when she'd push my hair out of my face. I cried a lonely cry that made my chest hollow and weary and desiccated like an abandoned nest. It was the loneliness of the reality of living in a treatment center. It was true and deep. I cried some more until the crying ran out and I remembered that Francie had said she hoped to get a visit for us. Then I looked up and said, "Thanks."

She smiled. "So since you're here at Castlerock, maybe we better find a way to deal with your anger. I want you to take notice of when you're *not* angry and what things you're doing when you feel that loose feeling in your wrists. It won't work all the time, but if you start noticing the things that make you feel that water feeling, you'll be able to calm yourself down better.

"Like I said, it won't be all the time. You're still going to get angry. So for next week, the next time you get a cuss sheet, because let's be honest—" she winked over the top of her glasses "—you're going to get one between now and then. So next time you get one, I want you to write about the word 'promise.' Then just for fun, look up a swear word too and write about what you find."

I had no idea why, but I felt better. I didn't worry about my mom. I thought about that watery loose feeling in my wrists and it helped. Staff was waiting to take me back to the cottage. It was a sunny Thursday and I swung my arms, and spun, walking backward, then forward all the way back. I was light as air.

That night I heard another girl awaken next door. She was new, wide-eyed, small, scared. Although she was a couple of years older than I, she didn't act it and while no one knew what'd happened to her, we could all tell it was pretty bad. She'd come with her hair really snarly and she had scabs on her scalp. She had a far-reaching stare and didn't say much. That night, I lay staring up at the ceiling, listening to staff talk to her, trying to calm her down. It wasn't working. They didn't get it. They couldn't get it.

Most of the staff were nice enough but they were young and hadn't lived the lives we had. No one had ever made them drink Drano the way that boy in the cottage across the way had. They didn't sport scars the whole world could see that their parents had given them. They didn't need erasers to feel secure.

Neither did I.

But I did understand waking up screaming from dreams that sweat through my spine. I knew nightmares.

So I went to her room, sat against the wall outside her doorway and said, "I have nightmares too. I wake up screaming sometimes. People tease me about it but I don't care. I dream about the man who tried to rape me and in my dreams it happens all over again. I don't know what you're dreaming about, or why you have bad dreams, but if you want to talk about it, I'm Seffra and I sleep next door." My back slid up the pastel-painted wood as I stood and shuffled back to my room.

The staff doesn't always approve of this, but this over night worker didn't say anything.

The next night, the new girl heard me screaming and came to my door. "We could talk in the living room."

We talked for a while about music and then went back to bed. She liked country and I hated it. She was preppy. I was somewhere between hip-hop and grunge. But I liked having a friend enough that I let it slide.

Her name was Angelique. As the look of a wild animal began to fade, the eyes of a person emerged. Her scalp healed and she started brushing her hair again. She was pretty and quiet and scared easily. She was significantly smaller than I was even though she was older. I was about average for my age. I was taller than most of the boys but not gawky. She was birdlike and dainty. She liked things orderly and wore pink almost every day. We didn't have much in common beyond our dreams, but over time, it was enough.

The overnight worker from Thursday to Sunday let us hang out but the front of the week worker didn't. One Friday night after we'd been friends for a couple of weeks Angelique told me what had happened to her.

She'd been molested by an older cousin. It went on for years. She told her parents but they didn't believe her. They left her alone with him over and over again. Last year, she'd gotten her period and shortly after that he'd gotten her pregnant. She wasn't sure what to do since her parents didn't believe her. She didn't tell them this time. She hid it from everyone beneath baggy sweatshirts and sweatpants. She gave birth at home by herself. She was fourteen years old.

She hadn't known to tie off the umbilical cord before cutting it and so the baby bled out. She hadn't meant to kill him, she just didn't know what she was doing. She was scared and too young and without help. The worst part was that she'd loved the baby. She'd done the best she could and it wasn't enough. He'd died. And her parents blamed her.

Castlerock was her fifth placement. She'd been to a group home, juvie, a foster home, another treatment center, and now here. Her parents gave up their rights and she was on her own.

"So where will you live after here?"

She shrugged. "I'll be here until they kick me out and then I'll live somewhere else." She looked me square in the face. "But if my parents wanted me, I'd run away in a heartbeat and be home again."

"I miss my mom like crazy," I admitted. "Sometimes I think if I could get back to her, everything would be fine."

"So why don't you?" she asked.

"It's complicated. My mom's got to prove she can take care of me." She nodded. "I'm sorry."

She told me the courts never let kids like us go home. "If I were you, I'd run."

I told her more about Dante. About stabbing him and how he'd died later and how I wasn't sure what the police were going to do about it. I left out the stuff about Kara, only telling her what Dante actually did and what I did.

She didn't judge me or seem to think I was a maniac or anything, but tears were in her eyes.

"Seffra, you're a girl of promise. You're brave, and that man deserved what he got. If I'd had a knife even once with my cousin, I'd have killed him over and over again. You did the right thing."

She still thought I should run though. But I hadn't taken up a knife against her cousin, it had been Dante. I thought about the part I hadn't told her, the part about Kara. I wondered if I should run like she said. If I knew where my mom was and how to get there, I might do it. My mom probably would've run if she were in my shoes.

I thought about the things Kara and I had done, the way we'd kissed and touched and I knew part of Dante's death had been my fault. Still, it felt good to have a friend who took my side, a friend who believed I'd done the right thing. It felt good to tell another person how he'd tried to rape me and I'd defended myself. It felt good to be right and to have done the right thing. Maybe I had.

I told Angelique about how my dad shot my mom and how my mom had taken off with me afterwards to keep us together.

"I really wish I knew where she was, because I just know she'd take me and we'd run and she'd make sure we could stay together and that they wouldn't get me for what happened with Dante. But I don't know how to find her, and if I get caught running, it would make me look like I did something wrong. But I didn't. That asshole deserved it." I shrugged. "So I guess I better try to do the treatment thing."

In that moment, I believed I'd done the right thing. I wouldn't have been better off getting pregnant or dealing with the rape. Fuck Kara. I'd defended myself, I *was* brave, and I *was* strong. I would get better. I'd try anyway.

9

I kept paying attention to the times when I wasn't angry. I felt good when I was helping Angelique. And I felt good when I was drawing. I'd always felt good drawing and doing artwork. When I was with my mom and we traveled, I always brought a notebook along to draw in the car or to pass the time if my mom left me alone for a long time. When I was mad or sad or bored I drew and it helped me stay calm and focused. I liked looking at things and imagining what they'd look like as sketches and I loved the art museum my mom had taken me to in Chicago.

I tried to stick to doing things that made me feel calm and useful. I had a good week at school. I tried in class. I listened and wasn't disrespectful. I didn't even cuss much.

It was hard though too. Angelique's comment about running back home stayed with me and it was hard because all I wanted was to be with my mom. But I knew I couldn't be so I tried to push that away and just remember the feeling in my wrists like Francie said. It worked most of the time and I was doing well.

I bragged about it to encourage myself. "Hey Miss, I'm on green today," I said to the art teacher in the hallway.

"Really? That's wonderful to hear," she said tucking a stack of papers under one arm.

"Yup," I said proudly.

"So does that mean you're headed to Friday Fun this week?"

I made a face.

She knit her brow and barked, "Walk with me."

When we got to the art room, she pulled two stools down and set them next to the marked up table. The metal clanged against the tile floor as she set them down. The top of the table was flecked with old, dried clay and countless paint stains. I ran my hand across the rough surface and smelled my palm. It smelled like pottery and paint and sandalwood. The whole room smelled like art and earth and paint. It was light in that room and dusty. The room had floor to ceiling windows that let in tons of light. Dust hung in the light streaming in that day.

The room was full of random supplies: a few dozen empty tissue boxes stacked in one corner, bottles of paint in plastic totes, in another corner newspaper unfolded and stacked three feet high. My stool was uneven and I rocked back and forth on the unsteady legs.

"What's the story with you and Friday Fun, huh?" she asked.

I used a fingernail to pry some clay loose and shrugged.

"Do you not want to go? I hear they're going to the movies this week. Who doesn't like movies?"

I didn't know what to say. I shrugged again.

"Eh, whatever floats your boat, Chiquita. You don't like movies or Friday Fun, that's fine with me." Her eyes narrowed and she reached a finger out pointing it at me.

"Not doing well in treatment, though? *That*'s not fine with me. I want to see you get out of here."

"Why is everyone in such a hurry to see me get out of here? What's the deal with that?"

"Ah, that's it. You're self-sabotaging. You don't *want* to get out of here, is that it?"

I protested but her mind was made up. Of course I wanted out. I hated it. I hated that I had to go to school every morning. I hated that I got in trouble for cussing. I hated that there were staff everywhere. I hated that I couldn't listen to loud music. I hated that I couldn't go to my room when I wanted or take a shower for as long as I wanted. I hated that there was a basket with my name on it that had all my generic crappy *hygiene* supplies and that I couldn't rummage around in the cupboards or eat a snack in my bed even though there was food all the time. I hated that even though I couldn't eat whenever I wanted, I was gaining weight like mad and my pants didn't fit anymore. I even hated that Alison would probably buy me new ones if I asked. I hated basically everything. Why would I want to stay there?

"That's not true. I hate it here. I just want to go home with my mom but they won't let me."

"So you're stuck here then, that it?"

"I mean, I guess I could run."

"You better stop that kinda talk, little girl," she warned.

"I know. But Angelique said she'd run if she could go home."

"Oh, 'Angelique said' huh?" She raised her voice. "That must be true then, right? Clearly she's made all the best choices and so you should listen to *her*."

"No." I knit my brow. "I don't know," I stammered.

"Do you know how many places that girl's lived? Do you want to live in six or seven different homes? You think you hate it here? Ask her about what her homes have been like." She goaded, "Whatever you want to happen with your mom, getting in with kids running and doing dumb stuff isn't going to help you." She wasn't letting up or going easy on me at all. "I'm calling up to your homeroom. I think you should stay here for a while."

She picked up the phone and called up to my class and asked my staff if she could have me stay in her room to work on a project over lunch. No, I wasn't in trouble, not yet. She half-heartedly glared at me. She just thought it might be good for me, she explained.

She settled me down to a project she needed help with. She wanted bubble letters of the names of all the kids in the school for some project. I drew names for a long time and didn't even bother to eat the meal she brought me.

Sabrina walked by and gave me her usual psycho-smile. "What you doin' in here? You on the run?"

"Maybe," I said.

The art teacher made a face.

Then thinking of what she'd said about Angelique and how much better I felt now drawing, I tightened the corner of my mouth and shook my head no.

"She's helping me, nosy-pants. Go to your homeroom where you're supposed to be," she told Angelique.

When Sabrina was gone, the art teacher said, "Why do you do that? You're tough. Why don't you just tell kids like Sabrina and Angelique to stuff it when they try to pull you down with them? Running, swearing, you're better than all that, Seff."

My mom called me that.

I felt sheepish. "I just want friends. Besides, my mom liked to party and so do those girls. I don't want to be better than anybody. I just want to fit in and hang out. I want my mom to like me."

"Well, and look where that got your mom." She was relentless. "The person she loves most is in here and she's got problems. Is that what you want? Because you can go that way too, girl. It's easy." She took a breath and quieted a little. "I bet your mom likes how strong you are. I bet she wants better for you than parties and friends who only bring you down."

We both sat quietly for a moment before she gestured toward what I was working on, changing the subject. "That looks great. You could be an artist, you know. Or you could just use art to help you in life instead of choosing crappy friends or running away." She looked right into my face. Then she rolled her eyes and said. "Go on back now. And don't get in any more trouble. Stay on green, okay?"

She let go a breath, and, exasperated, added, "I tell you what. If you stay on green and can go to Friday Fun, I'll let you choose if you want to stay here and do a project instead of going to the movies.

Just this once though; don't think it's because I like you or anything. Now get out of here." She waved her hand and then she picked up the phone on her desk to call and let them know I was on my way back to class and I tried to hide my smile as I headed out the door.

10

F rancie was true to her word about getting a visit set up with my mom. Even though I didn't think my mom could sober up the way they wanted, I was wrong. Either that or she found a way to cheat the system and pretend to be sober. Whatever the case, I was going to see her. Our visit would be supervised and with Francie, my therapist there, but I'd get to see my mom.

Before the first visit I was nervous and excited. Angelique did my hair and I wore makeup too. I couldn't concentrate all morning and kept reminding my teachers that I had to leave to go to my visit at 1:30. They hadn't forgotten and could tell that I was thinking of nothing else. I was so nervous and excited. I had built it up that this would solve all my problems. I'd be able to go home soon and it'd be like the whole thing had never happened. Francie tried to prepare me and tell me it wouldn't be that way, but I couldn't help myself. The thing about parents is you always expect them to come and make it all better, even if they pretty much never do.

We met in Francie's office. Francie had lamps all over in her office and she kept the overhead lighting turned off. She burned sandalwood candles all day and had a loveseat on one wall, an overstuffed chair on another, and her desk and office chair on the third. On the wall was a painting I stared at a lot during sessions. The moon was in the top right corner above a sandy beach with ocean waves in the foreground. The beach was in purples and gave way to the blues of the waves before becoming white around the moon.

Francie sat in her office chair and I sat in the overstuffed chair when my mom came up.

When I saw my mom, I was flooded with too many emotions to count: love, anxiety, frustration, anxiety, anger, need. I stood up. As much as I wanted to, though I couldn't run to her the way I'd thought I would. I didn't fall into her arms; I was too angry.

"Hey there, baby!" she said in her tempting drawl. "Ain't you gonna give me a hug after all I been through to see you?"

My feet were stuck. I didn't want her to be disappointed. I didn't want her to leave me again, but what the hell? After all *she'd* been through? Had she had to kill someone I didn't know about to get here?

Finally my feet came unstuck and I went over and hugged her. My anger pushed away for a few moments and I felt the rush of my mother's smell, and how much I loved her and I was sad with need and longing. I pushed sad back and for that moment felt like forever could wrap me in a blanket and keep me safe and warm. I never, never wanted it to end.

She looked good. Her pale skin was smooth; her hair shone, and she looked healthy. She'd gained a little weight, probably because she wasn't doing drugs anymore and was actually eating, and it looked fantastic. I sniffled against her shoulder and she leaned back, brushing the hair out of my eyes and looking at my face.

"You look like your father." I wasn't sure how to take that. "You always have. You're gettin' so big and grown-lookin'. Ah just can't believe how long it's been. My God. I missed you." She pulled her sunglasses off and I greedily took in her scar. The thing I knew that others didn't. The part of her under and behind and hidden. It was mine.

We exchanged some pleasantries and then Francie, my therapist, took over.

"Ms. Morgan, other than how Seffra has grown, did you notice anything else when you first saw her today?" Francie asked.

My mom didn't like her question, didn't like Francie. I could tell. She didn't like people involved in our business.

"Why, what ever do you mean? I don't like this psychobabble talk. If you have somethin' to say, you oughta just come right out and say it." She blinked several times and replaced her sunglasses.

Francie adjusted her position and took a breath. "There's no need to be defensive; it's my job to help you and Seffra develop a better relationship and one of the ways I do that is by asking questions. You seem uncomfortable with me. Is there something we can do to work on that?"

My mom made a face. Francie was good and my mom wouldn't be able to just pull off her usual tricks to get out of things.

My mom sat back and crossed her arms. "I suppose I am a bit uncomfortable. I never had someone watchin' me and my daughter while we talk and it's a bit strange."

"That's understandable Ms. Morgan," she said, resolute. "You should know first and foremost that I am committed to helping you and your daughter make your relationship better. I'm not here to make your life harder, but the work of improvement will be challenging."

My mother actually nodded. If she was faking, she was fooling me.

"The reason I asked you that question is that I noticed Seffra seemed to get uncomfortable when she first saw you and I wondered if you noticed. I wonder how you felt about that?"

"I'm sure I don't know what you're talking about." She flipped her hair aside and adjusted her position.

"Let me back up. If therapy is going to help you and Seffra to improve your relationship, everyone's going to have to feel comfortable talking here. We're going to have to let Seffra know that this is a safe place to say what she needs to say and that feelings will be handled here. So a good place to start might be rules."

We worked on setting up ground rules for our therapy. Rules like for now we wouldn't talk about what happened, and that no one would leave in the middle of a session, and that no one would name call. Francie made sure it was some place we could talk about things and then she returned to my discomfort. I told my mom about how I'd been feeling, about how I hadn't expected it, but felt angry when she walked in.

She held up her end of the bargain and didn't call me any names or get up and leave. But I knew how she felt, and what she thought. She wasn't all smiles and fun anymore and we didn't have the best visit ever. It didn't solve everything. Also, I realized that I'd changed a lot in the past months and it would time before we were tight like we used to be. I told her I loved her when she left and she promised to call.

When I got back to the cottage, everyone asked how the visit was in high-pitched, eager voices. I said fine and quickly changed the subject. No one pressed. I was allowed room time and I took advantage of the chance to take a long nap. I awoke with a jolt of anxiety and pulled out a notebook to draw in. It didn't calm me, even when I tried to think my wrists into being loose. I focused all my energy and commanded them to be loose and easy but it didn't work. I got more anxious.

That night I couldn't sleep. I kept thinking that I'd ruined things with my mom and that she'd probably never call me again. I hated Francie for not making it all go right and for having the idea in the first place. I hated Social Services for taking me away from my mom. I hated Castlerock for every single minute I had to spend there. I wanted to go home. I wanted to go back to the way things were.

I rethought every word I'd spoken. I regretted not telling my mom how proud I was for the work she'd done to get sober. I forgot to say thank you for coming to see me. I didn't compliment how nice she looked. I didn't even notice what she was wearing. I didn't ask her what music she was listening to. I went on and on with all the things I should have done/asked/said differently. I forgot to beg her to come back. Maybe if I begged.

I thought how my mom probably really felt about what I'd said. I knew she wouldn't love me if I was angry with her, she never had. She cut off affection in a heartbeat. It was brutal. I tossed and turned in my regret, my sheets twisting me up, I kicked them toward the foot of the bed. Then I thought about all the good times I'd had with my mom and longed for those times. I thought about how much fun she could be.

I remembered one time when they cut the lights off at our house because mom hadn't paid the bills. I remember I was scared but my mom had said, "Don't you worry. It ain't nothin' a party can't fix, baby."

We lit candles and then she pulled out an industrial size roll of bubble wrap. Her boyfriend at the time worked in a packaging plant and brought it home. It was something like six feet tall and a big bundle around. We moved the coffee table out of the way in the living room and unrolled it. It was a foot deep across the entire floor. We jumped up and down on it laughing until we were exhausted and lying in the pile. It was loud and hilarious and we didn't care who we annoyed with it. Plus we were warm.

I thought of times she'd be getting ready to go out with her friends. What a good mood she'd be in. She was unstoppable in her spiked heels and her sexy lip gloss. She'd crank up the Jackson 5 and we'd dance around the apartment singing at the top of our lungs. She'd put makeup on me and even give me a squirt of her perfume. In those moments her beauty was contagious. I became a luxurious star who'd be watched and followed. We'd be big.

11

I seemed to wake a few days later.

Francie was trying to talk to me about the visit. I was still pissed at her for what happened at the visit with my mom.

"How're you feeling about the visit with your mom?"

"Fine." My arms were folded and I didn't look at her. I didn't look at the painting with the moon and the water either. I could hear her uncross and recross her legs, repositioning.

I unfolded my arms and looked at my fingers. I cracked my middle knuckles, one after the other, and glanced up.

Francie was wearing her glasses and a pleated skirt and a cream-colored button-down blouse. Her long legs were crossed with her knees lying loose to one side and she wore navy high heels and stockings.

"Your body language is saying that you don't feel fine."

I didn't say anything.

"You're crossing your arms tightly around yourself and avoiding eye-contact. You are slumped over and making your body tight and small. How does that feel?"

"Okay, I guess. I mean, I'm a little—"

"Closed off?"

I searched her. I didn't know what *closed off* meant exactly. I found myself looking at her to try to figure it out.

"Closed off, like you don't want me to talk to you or you can't take in more information right now. But since we started talking about it, you've opened up."

I had scooted forward in my seat and uncrossed my arms. I thought about what she said.

"Actually, I'm confused. I uh, I don't want you to think I'm nutso but uh...Never mind."

"What is it, Seffra? What's confusing? The visit? I can see why that would be confusing."

"No, not the visit." My mouth tightened, and I looked back and forth searching for the right words. "It's just that I get confused and well...I get mixed up about when stuff happened, is all."

"You get mixed up about the order of things that happened a while ago, or things that just happened?"

I noticed the pen in her hand. "Never mind, I'm sure it's nothing."

She set her pen and pad of paper down and looked at me. "Seffra, it's okay to tell me. I'm not going to think you're crazy. I do need to know what's going on with you if I'm going to help you. Neither one is abnormal. It's pretty typical for kids who have been traumatized to get mixed up about time and order. I just want to know which it is."

I gathered my strength and then said, "Both. But mainly, sometimes I don't remember, like, going from one class to another." I searched her face.

"So you space out between classes. Is that new?"

"Okay, it's more than just between classes. I don't remember what happened since I saw my mom." I sped the last bit out. Then, I teared up and didn't meet her gaze. "I'm sure that's not normal, but I guess I just needed you to know." I was crying hard now.

Francie reached out with a box of tissue and I took one.

"Okay, it's alright to have a lot of feelings about that lost time. It's also very normal to lose time. It happens to a lot of people who've had experiences like yours. Their mind protects them by sort of going on autopilot for a while. In most people it happens more often in times of stress or if there's something that reminds the person of what happened. It will get better. In the mean time, when you lose time, what do you do?"

"What do you mean?"

"I mean, how you piece that time back together is important. It's a good strategy to try to stay calm. Think again of how it feels in your body to be calm. If you can get your body calmed down, sometimes it helps your mind to calm down and you can remember things. Or you'll calm down and listen and be able to figure them out. Another thing you can do is tell a staff member that this is happening to you. This happens to lots of kids and the staff can help. That's why you're here. So people can help you when *normal* things like this happen."

I was so relieved I cried and smiled at the same time. Through blowing my nose, I asked, "Can we talk about the visit now? I'm ready."

"Sure." She paused and my breathing became slowed and even and I wasn't mad at her anymore. She continued, "Most kids have a lot of feelings after a visit like yours. Many kids feel sad or angry or tired or all of those things. It can be confusing. I'm here to help you and your mom develop a better relationship in the future."

Even though most of me knew better, I couldn't help being drawn in by the sparkle of a relationship and the future. I eased into it. "I do feel all that stuff," I admitted. I admitted to the sleepiness and the anger and the regrets and all the things I thought about. I admitted I'd been having trouble sleeping.

We talked some more about what I could do when I was angry or sad and she told me it was normal to feel that way, *okay* to feel that way, and that it didn't mean not seeing my mom anymore. I was so relieved. The time I'd lost was normal. I'd had a good cry. I had some things I could *do* to figure it all out.

"I think you need to see your mom more. I am recommending to your caseworker that you continue to see your mom in therapy sessions with me but that you also see her here for short unsupervised visits a couple of times a week."

I couldn't believe it. She wanted me to see my mom more. I wiggled and struggled to stay in my seat for the rest of the session.

12

I fantasized constantly about how good my life would be with my mom when I got out. I put all my hope in her being sober and us living together again. There'd be plenty to eat and without drinking and drugs, our life would be perfect. We'd have food and money and new friends, nice clothes and good music. They'd never cut the lights off. Any time I was getting annoyed with Castlerock, I'd just picture how perfect my life was going to be when it was all over.

There was a time when a kid was throwing a fit about having to add his last name to a paper.

"We use first *and* last names on papers," I barely overheard in the background of my own thoughts.

I zoned out while the class listened to the implied threats of staff. As the confrontation continued, I thought instead of what I'd pack and where we'd go when my mom came to rescue me. I pictured getting in a nice big car and driving on smooth pavement to Indiana, or Wisconsin, or Florida. Yes, Florida. Someplace warm and southern. Our lives there would be perfect. I pictured us with toothy smiles, strolling along a boardwalk licking our ice cream.

I'd begun seeing my mom more and it had been good. She'd bring McDonald's and we'd hang out on the picnic benches while she told me about her new friends and how hard she was working to stay sober. She'd hug me and brush my hair back with her hand and kiss my forehead. She talked about her job at the front desk of a motel and talked about her coworkers.

"Things are gonna be better for us, baby, promise." She emphasized *promise*. She told me about her new boyfriend. I basked in the attention and didn't say much.

But then something happened. I couldn't remember anyone telling me specifics: but visits would be stopped for a while. I'd lost time again and came to in therapy.

"I don't want to press you. Just know that you can speak freely in here about your feelings." I was in Francie's office. "I'm here to help you process this."

"I don't want to talk about my fucking feelings. I'm fine. I told you I was fine before and I'm still fine now. So leave. Me. Alone."

I lost more time. I just seemed to go in a fog and I'd come to in a new place, trying to figure out what had happened. This time, I lost weeks. I tried staying calm like Francie told me. I tried but when I loosed my wrists, I got so angry I'd dig my fingernails into my palms until I started screaming, releasing all that anger on everyone around me like emotional volcanic vomit. Then I'd lose more time.

I had snapshots of being told again by staff that visits were temporarily cut off with my mom and screaming in my room. I couldn't tell if any of the snapshots had really happened or if they were dreams. I remembered lying on the shower floor freaking out about slime from the floor getting on me and needing to scrub it off. I remembered scrubbing with rocks much like in the dreams I had in the hospital. I remembered hearing a voice saying that I was going to run out of hot water soon and telling me to get out. Somehow, though, I knew the part about not seeing my mom was real.

"Seffra, you with us?"

"Huh? Yeah, whatever," I said, wiping my eyes.

I looked around: florescent lights, green chalkboard on wheels with the words "Learn, Grow, DO," desks in a *U*-shape. I was in Independent Living Skills Group. I didn't give a shit about *Independent Living Skills Group*. This was where we learned to tie our shoes and wash our clothes and take the bus. In case anyone hadn't noticed I had *tons* of independent living skills.

"Today in group we're going to learn to take the bus to and from the library. You guys will plan the route and then we'll actually take the bus and go to get our own library cards." More of that chipper shit. I rolled my eyes.

"I thought the bus to prison is free and the warden arranged whether or not you get to work in the library," I said, leaning so far back, my desk tipped slightly.

"Excuse me?"

"You heard me," I leaned forward and let the desk slam back down again.

"Well, Seffra, I thought you liked to read and you'd be pleased to be working on this project."

That's another thing about staff in treatment centers: they seem to all have this overly sweet voice that you *know* is bullshit, but they insist on pretending with it anyway. The worst part is the way you can't disprove it. Open hostility is something you can tell another person about, but this bizarre marzipan surface with arsenic bitter just underneath can only be sensed, not proven. I wonder if that's how people end up in those jobs: they have that dripping, falsetto-voice and so some school counselor along the way somewhere says, "Hey, you have the perfect demeanor to work in a residential treatment center." Almost like those people you meet from time to time that have radio voices and you *know* someone or a couple of someone's told them to get into radio.

"Please," I said stretching out the *E* and rolling my eyes. "There's no way I'd do this project. It's a waste of my time," I glanced sideways and nodded at the other kids.

Then another staff member intervened, a less phony one who'd had about enough of my attitude and said so.

"Really? I'm so sorry, did you have something better to do?" He stepped closer to my desk.

I looked at the other side of the class and nodded at those kids. "Anything would be better than this." The other kids avoided my gaze.

"Just why exactly do you feel this is so beneath you, princess Seffra?" He stood in front of me, leaning over and putting a hand on the desk.

"Any idiot can figure out a bus schedule and if you're *really* too stupid to do that, then you can just go to the nearest bus stop with some change and *ask* the bus driver." I stood up. His face was close to mine now and it spurred me on. I was on a roll now. "Besides, you're probably just going to pick the books we *have* to check out for us anyway. I'm sure you won't let us check out what we want. You'll stand over us the whole time and listen to every word. Shit, you'll probably read over our shoulders the whole ride back here. You don't let us do anything we want. You treat us like a bunch of *babies!*" I waved my arms around gesturing wildly; I was fired up. "You know what? Fuck this. I'm outa here," I said and went for the door.

Todd, the staff member, followed me into the hallway where we were met by another staff.

"Whoa, let's just calm down. Take some breaths. Do you want to go to the chill room?" Todd stood in front of me, his palms held out wide.

"Man, fuck you and your chill room!" I yelled.

"You know you can't get that loud out here. I can't let you disturb class going on in those rooms." The sweet surface was cracking and under it was unforgiving concrete. He stepped closer to me, his hands still out wide.

"Fuck class! Nobody learns anything in this hellhole anyway! You people don't know how to teach. You just hand us stupid worksheets about our *feelings*. This is bullshit. Here's some *feelings*." And I flipped them off and tried taking a step backward. Both the staff stepped closer. They were closing in. Now both their hands were held out wide, like they were dogcatchers narrowing in on me.

I was mad. Beyond mad. I didn't know what to do with all my mad.

"Seffra, we know it's hard for you being here. We know it's hard when you don't have a family, but…"

That was the final straw; I lost it. "*Fuck you! I had a family until you fucking social workers took it away from me!*" I screamed. I grabbed the fire extinguisher and threw it at the guy. He ducked and before I knew it, I was face down on the ground. I fought and bucked. I tried to reach my fingernails into whoever was holding my wrists. I could hardly move.

"*Let go of me!*" I shouted, my voice scratchy. I saw someone ahead of me through a dusty white fog and recognized my teacher.

"*They're hurting me!*" I screamed. "*I can't breathe!*" I must've pulled the pin because the extinguisher discharged, and there was nitrogen powder everywhere.

Then I heard her whisper a question, "Do you need anything?"

"*Yes, fucking help me!*"

But she wasn't talking to me. She didn't give a shit about me; she was talking to the staff restraining me. This fueled my fury even more. I had a lot of adrenaline and I fully intended to use it. I squirmed and fought and at some point lost touch with reality. I didn't know if I was fighting at Castlerock or back on the sofa bed. I slammed my head, scratched anything I could and thrashed for all I was worth.

As the flashback intensified, I smelled whisky, and fought even harder. At one point I got my arm free and I punched someone. I twisted to get out of it and dislocated my shoulder. It didn't matter. I couldn't feel anything. All I knew was panic and fear and survival. I was being attacked and I had to get out of it.

13

The restraint lasted fifty-one minutes. The school's director walked by and told them to let me go. Normally they restrained until we calmed, until we complied. But it was obvious that I wasn't calming down and that I was hurt.

A lockdown order came over the loudspeaker. Locks on all the doors clicked into place.

The director quietly told them, "Let her go and get out of the way."

Adrenaline coursed through me as I ran out of the building. Once outside though, I grew dizzy, disoriented. Shock set in, and I fainted.

Police and an ambulance came. I heard my mother's warning: *You don't say a word to the law.* The paramedics put me on a stretcher.

In voices small and faraway, I heard them discussing me. I felt the banging of the road and thought of the drive when I fractured my skull.

"What happened?"

"Independent Living Skills Group—she freaked."

That restraint had nothing to do with Independent Living. I knew how to do independence. It was depending on people I couldn't handle. They put an IV in and transported me to the hospital.

I awoke and recognized the antiseptic smell of hospital and the cool, crisp white sheet against my cheek. I had rug burns on my face from the indoor/outdoor carpet I'd fought against on the floor. My shoulder was in a sling and my head hurt. The pain felt right. I leaned into it and enjoyed the contrast of the cool sheet and my warm cheek, and the sting where they met. I lay feeling the sting for a long time.

My shoulder was sore when I moved it. I stretched it against the sling, then I pulled the IV out of my other arm. I pushed against my skin, watching the dot grow where the IV had been. The blood bubble in the crook of my arm expanded. I liked the way the dark red bubble grew. I liked the way my arm burned when I moved it in order to push against the IV hole. I wanted to see how big I could make the bubble before it would give in and split into a rivulet pouring down my wrist, dripping to the floor. But something was beeping and a nurse bustled in and replaced it while I lay back. I said nothing.

A numbing flushed cold through my veins and my mind grew fuzzy and comfortably blank. I slept and dreamed of nothing.

After what I'd guess was a few hours, the hospital psychiatrist came in to evaluate whether I could return or not, if I was safe enough or needed to be hospitalized.

I didn't even turn my head. "How are you feeling?"

I stayed silent. "Do you have feelings of hopelessness?"

I still didn't say anything.

"Do you feel like hurting yourself or someone else?"

They took my non-answers to mean that I needed to be hospitalized for a few days so they could evaluate me further. They had to make sure I wasn't *a danger to myself or others* before sending me back to Castlerock.

They drugged me up, which felt fine to me. I slept and slept. The drug fog was good; I couldn't see a single part of my real life through it. Which was necessary, because I didn't know what I would say my real life even was at that point. I'd been thinking my real life was the one with my mom. The one where she got better and took care of me. The one where everything that happened with Dante disappeared and I got to go back to the south side and skip school in the park and tell Boogie jokes. But if I couldn't even see my mom, was that really my life? As they lowered dosages and the fog slowly lifted, I wondered what my real life was. I hoped this wasn't it.

The psychiatrist checked my pupils. "Looking better today, I think." His accent was Indian.

"Do you have a dictionary by any chance?" I asked.

"You must be better if you are asking for a dictionary." He smiled. "I will see that a nurse bring one to you." I liked the way his t's sounded soft and round and the way his d's sounded like they might bounce.

I smiled.

He looked serious and held a finger up. "You know, the police are waiting on me to tell them you are ready to speak with them. But I think, not yet. Maybe tomorrow."

The psychiatrist held the police off for another day, but they were keen on interviewing me some more about Dante's death. I was incredibly nervous. I didn't know if they had new information from Kara. I suspected that was the reason why they wanted to talk to me some more.

The real reason was because they'd gone over all the information from all the interviews and wanted to finalize the investigation but had some outstanding questions about the information I'd provided. They weren't totally sold on self-defense. One of the investigators believed I'd attacked Dante and lied about why. I couldn't see my mom because the police needed the interview to be "clean." They didn't want me to get secretly coached by my mom about what to say.

The interview process was grueling and it was probably good that I was in the hospital instead of at Castlerock for it. They asked the same questions over and over again. I felt small in my hospital bed. There were only two officers, but it seemed like more with their formal navy suits looming dark above me. I swear the room was darker, like their uniforms sopped up the florescent light and dimmed the room to scare me into a confession.

"If you stabbed him in self-defense, why did you lie to us the first time we asked about his death?" the officer stepped closer to the bed.

"I didn't lie. I told you everything. Why do you keep asking me about lying?"

Well, maybe not *everything*. I never told them anything about Kara.

I'm not a liar. Never have been. Sure, I'll steal something from time to time, and I'll sign my mom's name to go on a field trip when she's too drunk to sign it herself, but I don't lie.

But they kept coming back to this point about how I'd lied about the stabbing. They'd ask me the same questions but worded differently, trying to trip me up.

"So let me get this straight, where did you stab him?" He paced and pointed up as he asked, as if the answer to his question were hidden in the lights.

"It was in the living room, on the couch. I told you. He tried to rape me and I stabbed him."

"And how many times did you stab him?"

"Twice. After the second time, I got out of there as fast as I could." I held a pillow in front of me and crushed it smaller into myself.

"But you told us the stabbing was in the bathroom?" he looked at me and cocked his head, challenging my story.

"I never said that."

"Why would you say it happened in the bathroom?" he stepped closer to the bed.

"I didn't say that." I thrust the pillow to the side and sat forward. "I didn't say that."

They just kept trying to get me to say I did it somewhere else.

"I have the recording right here, shall I play it?"

Go ahead, asshole.

I glared, not answering.

He set the recorder on my food tray and pressed the button. It clicked and the recording came on. "How many times?" Then quiet, then in a lower voice, "Let the record indicate the subject held up two fingers." Then: "How did his blood get on your nightgown?" There were jostling papers, and then a gagging sound and then my voice saying, "In the bathroom."

It was my voice but that's not what I'd said. How had they twisted it? I didn't understand.

I choked a little. "But, that's not what happened. That's not what I said. I don't understand." I was having trouble breathing. "It was him. I didn't do anything wrong. Everyone said I didn't do anything wrong. I don't understand." I buried my face in the hospital bed and sobbed. But they didn't let up.

"So why did you lie to us?"

"I didn't. I don't know. I don't understand," I sobbed.

"There's no question that you lied. You just heard yourself. So why lie? Do you have something to hide? How about you tell us the real story now?"

I stopped answering. I pulled a pillow over my face and writhed in my bed.

Uncle Phin, help me. Make them stop. I don't understand. I can't take this anymore. Help.

Finally, a nurse came in. "Excuse me, Officers, may I please speak with you in the hallway?" She smiled and blinked.

The nurse must've kicked them out or something because they didn't come back in.

They left but the idea of what they were saying hung in my mind. I played the recording over and over in my mind. *How did his blood get on your nightgown?* Then I was gagging and then me *in the bathroom.* What was I talking about?

I turned it over and over trying to figure it out. I couldn't think of anything else because I was convinced that the police wouldn't believe me and that I was going to jail for murdering Dante if I didn't figure out why I'd said that. I couldn't believe that I'd lied. Why would I say it happened in the bathroom?

If they charged me, I'd never get to go home. It wouldn't matter that my mom was trying. It wouldn't matter that she was sober or had a job or a plan for how to keep us together. She'd help if I could just stop ruining everything. Why had I said that?

Alison came to visit me later that day. Her hair was tied back and her face was stern. She skipped the niceties and straightaway said, "I'm worried about you."

I wondered what all Alison knew about the police investigation. Would she tell me if the police were going to charge me? I thought she would. She might even tell me if they'd talked to Kara. But I mostly didn't want to know. It felt too dark to find out.

I barely looked up. "I just want my mom."

"I told you that you couldn't see your mom until the police investigation was complete." She looked at me, puzzled. "Remember? I said it was only temporary and you could see her when it was over. That I was sorry. Remember?"

But I didn't remember. I shook my head.

She adjusted her skirt and I thought, *She looks like shit.* I thought she should fix herself up in the bathroom or something and then I remembered why I'd said what I'd said to the police.

"The police," I said sitting up. "I told them the bathroom because I was talking about throwing up. They thought I meant that I stabbed Dante there, but I was saying that's where I'd gone to throw up the first time he, you know, touched me. We were talking about different things and now they think I lied. Now they'll never let me see my mom."

I felt my already puffy face flush and I wished I could hide it in the dark. I hadn't brushed my hair since the morning I'd come in. I tugged at a strand, willing it to be less greasy. Then I pulled it back in a ponytail while trying to look at the floor, snapping the tie on and then stealing a glance at Alison. Her brow was knit and I wasn't sure what that could mean.

"You have to help me. You have to tell them," I begged. "Please, I'm desperate."

She put a hand on my shoulder.

"I know I screwed up." I was resolute though. "I didn't lie. I didn't do anything wrong. I just want my mom. Why won't this all just go away so I can be with my mom?"

Alison waited until I finished. She looked serious, almost stern and she said, "I will call and try and talk to the police for you, I promise."

And then a nurse came in and gave me something and I slept.

I lost a day or so to sleep and fog. But when I came to, there was a dictionary next to me in the bed and a small notebook. The word *promise* still swirled in my head, like it was being brought up my roots but not making its way to my leaves. My limbs and mind felt loose with a lack of resolve. Picking up the huge volume seemed too large a feat. I could hardly bear to move that far. I lazily twisted and flopped myself over and pressed my finger into the indent of the *P*-section. I opened to the page where I found:

Promise-verb something that one will definitely do, give, or arrange something; undertake or declare that something will happen.

My mom had promised all kinds of things. Sometimes she'd promise she was coming back soon and it would really take her days. Sometimes she'd promise to pay the bills or buy food but instead I'd find her passed out with the electricity turned off and empty cupboards. She promised to stop drinking a lot but of course she never did. The one promise she always kept, though, was that she'd find a way to keep us together. If it weren't for keeping us together, I'd think she didn't know what the word meant.

Against all reason, I trusted that my mom would find a way. I trusted that Alison would talk to the police. And against my better judgment, I felt a little hope creep in.

Alison came back to talk to me the next day.

"The doctors and nurses seem to think you'll be stable enough to get out of here in a day or so."

"Did you talk to the police?" I felt my whole body tense thinking of how I'd talked to the law when I shouldn't have. I shouldn't have said anything. I should have listened to my mom and refused to answer and just kept quiet.

"I did. Your psychiatrist told them that some inconsistencies in a victim's story are common, especially among children, and so the police have decided not to press charges against you in Dante's case. They're closing their case saying you acted in self-defense."

Alison's news should have made me feel better. But instead of listening to her, I tuned out the rest of what she said and instead the news churned around in my mind for a while. Kara wasn't going to ruin it all with lies about me and Dante. I wasn't my dad. I wasn't going to jail for what I'd done to Dante. The news kept flowing: *you acted in self-defense*, like all the water in my trunk was too much to be used. All that came out was the realization that I'd killed a man. No one faulted me, but still, I'd killed him. Because of me, another person was dead, and there was nothing that could undo that. I wanted to throw up.

I wanted my mom. I wanted to cry and cry on her lap. I wanted her to tell me she believed me too. That she thought I'd been brave, that she would take care of me now because I'd been good.

But I hadn't dared talk about Dante with my mom. He'd been her boyfriend after all and I didn't know what she thought about it all. It was in the rules of our visits that we not talk about Dante or what happened. We agreed to "table that topic for the time being." Francie's words.

I didn't table it so much as I shoved it into a tiny ball and tried to will it away. The sprout in my stomach dried out and shriveled up with the knowledge that the police ordeal was over and that no one else need ever hear about my disgusting feelings when he touched me. Still, while the pit shrunk, it persevered; it stayed, smaller now and rock hard.

"…we have to figure out where you're going live now." I tuned back in to what Alison was saying.

"Can I live with my mom? She's doing good, right? I want to live with her."

Alison tilted her head then shook it. "The courts are involved here. Which means for you to go back to living with your mom, a judge has to say it's okay first. And I don't think your mom has proven herself quite that clearly yet. She's doing well, yes, but…" She trailed off.

She wanted me to go back to Castlerock but they didn't have to take me back. I spaced back out and half-listened as she warned me about how I would have to do better if she could get me back into Castlerock. There was a waiting list, or someone was making her wait or something. I didn't care. If my mom and I couldn't be together, it was all the same to me.

"While getting you and your mom reunified is the goal—"

I snapped to. "So I get to see her again soon?" I interrupted.

"It's just that relapse is very common for people like your mom. She's doing well and that's good. But you need to—" She huffed and then said, "Seffra, don't you care about any of this? You need to *get* that you're in treatment. Your mom has to get better, yes. But you do too. How you're doing matters, and lately you haven't been doing too well."

I just wanted to know whether I could see my mom. Why was that such a terrible thing to ask?

I looked up cautiously. "Okay, I get it." I managed quietly.

Even though I didn't get it at all.

14

I went back to Castlerock. It was crap, really. My mom was sober and doing what they told her to do and I needed a place to be, so it should have been with my mom. But the courts don't work that way.

The courts don't reward good behavior, at least not quickly. They wait for confidence to falter and trip. When you're walking strong and steady, when your footing is stable, they say, "Let's wait and see what happens."

So I went back to Castlerock instead of home.

When I got back to Castlerock, the fight was all out of me. I was spent. The news of not going home with my mom, the time and energy spent going through everything that happened with Dante, and the medicine combined, congealed in my veins to make me slow and blank. I didn't look forward, just looked. The future was a slate grey dog that drooled and didn't mind its master. Tug on my leash, and I'd go where you led me.

The good news about this was that the adults thought I was doing great. I was almost always on green. I got all the privileges: TV time, extra desserts, field trips, etc. The bad news was I didn't care about any of it.

That is, I didn't care until Alison told me, "Great news: you're doing so well; we think you're ready to see your mom more. She's staying sober and doing most of what she's supposed to."

"Most of?"

"Well, she lost her job. But she's looking for another one and she's sober, so—"

"So I get to see her more?" I interrupted eagerly.

"Yup."

And *that* I did care about. She could get another job easy. Everyone liked my mom. Jobs were easy to come by; she just didn't really like to stay in any particular one for long, but she could keep *a* job. I knew she'd keep us together some way. I was going home.

I saw my mom about twice a week then. She came to the cottage on the weekends and we'd go for walks. We'd head out the door and down the sidewalk with the warm summer sun pink and yellow on the horizon, fooling us into thinking the evening was endless. The suburbs on a summer evening were pristine. You'd hear kids' high-pitched excited voices in backyards and the rhythmic squeal of swing springs on play sets.

In the city, there are cockroaches. And as the sun sets, they come out to forage for dinner. They scatter and scamper after dark. The setting sun is like a warning that this is about to happen. But in the suburbs I never saw a cockroach.

My mom and I would wander the winding roads, walking the debris-free sidewalks. She would chatter on about what she was doing and who had been a bitch and who had given her money for rent and she had another new boyfriend.

Woof, woof, WOOO! A large bark startled her.

"Woof woof," I answered the mastiff behind the privacy fence. "Don't worry boy, it's just us." I reached a hand through.

"Yah gonna lose that hand, girl," she said and pulled me back.

Even though she was wrong, that dog wouldn't have hurt me, I was happy. She didn't call me an idiot and she protected me. We walked on and I listened gladly to her chatter pick back up and watched the fences change back and forth between chain link and privacy, and picket, glad to have the sun on our backs.

We had therapy with Francie during the week at the main building. I sat in the chair and my mom sat in the loveseat, closest to the door. Francie sat in her office chair, the intermediary.

Some of the time we laughed and joked and I saw the nice mommy I'd always known. Like Uncle Phin helped get her out to see me. Other times he clearly left me in the lurch because she was defensive.

"You don't love your mama. And after all I done to get here to see you."

"That's silly, Mama. I love you like crazy. I do. It's just that you left me alone a lot and I'm trying to tell you how I felt about it." I leaned forward and held my arms out, trying to get her to listen.

"Girl, you know better than to lie like that. Y' wouldn't say these things in front ofa stranger, no offense doctor, if you loved me." Her arms were crossed and she looked at the door often when I said things like this.

It hurt so bad whenever she said I didn't love her. I didn't even care what else she said. It made me so insecure and afraid, all I cared about was fixing it and proving to my mother that I loved her.

Francie tried to keep things focused and usually she managed it pretty well; she was my individual therapist and also my advocate. She taught me how to use language to express what I needed it to say. I learned to deflect my mother's comments and keep the conversation focused by saying things like, "No, I didn't say I don't love you. I do love you, but when you told me I was stupid, it made me angry and sad and it made me feel worthless."

"Well, no matter what I say, I'm wrong. I guess I better just tell you I love you and be quiet." She rifled around in her purse, pulling her keys out.

This was actually a big improvement courtesy of Francie. My mom really didn't know what to do with it when I confronted her about our past.

In the beginning, she'd walk out and I'd know she didn't love me and would never love me again because of what I'd said. So Francie got her to at least stop leaving and tell me she loved me more. She still grabbed her keys, though, so I felt like she was about to leave, even though she didn't.

Her quiet was resentful and she avoided accountability for her part in our difficult life and the situation when she left me with the Crosbys. While the topic was still technically off limits, it got alluded to now and again. And always, my mom took no responsibility for it.

"I'm saying I spent a lot of time alone, mom."

"Weren't you tellin' me the other day how much you miss alone time? How these people are all over you and you can't do a thing by y'self?"

It was very frustrating because she was right, of course. I did hate that I never got to do anything by myself. But I also didn't like the way we'd lived where I had to do *everything* by myself. But I didn't know how to tell my mom that.

In individual therapy Francie and I talked. She spent time getting me to see how difficult this all was from my mother's perspective. If my mom took accountability for her part in what happened, she'd have to deal with the fact that if she'd taken care of me and faced the situation, I wouldn't have been alone with Dante at all. I would never have had to be in the situation that ended up costing him his life and me my mom.

Ultimately my mother's absence had a large part in the whole thing. Such a large part that she couldn't handle it. She was trying to hold down a regular job, come to weekly therapy, and go to drug abuse support groups. She had to be tested for drugs and alcohol weekly and still couldn't have her daughter home for months. I can admit that's a lot to try to handle at once. I tried to tell her thank you sometimes for all she was doing.

"I know you're working really hard, Mama. I really appreciate it. I do."

But my mom waved off those kinds of comments and changed the subject.

Francie tried not to let me dwell on it, because in her words, "You need to be the kid and let the adults be the adults." She knew I'd been an adult a lot of my life, and I wasn't one yet.

The problem was, I knew that Alison wasn't going to send me home with my mom if she thought my mom would put me in that position again. Alison would only believe my mom wouldn't put me in that position again if she took accountability for what happened. Alison told me as much.

Plus, I knew how to be an adult already and you can't just turn around and go backwards after being a grown up for all those years. We were making progress but we were still us. And that wasn't going to change as much as the judge and social worker and all those folks wanted.

And that truth scared me.

15

I was glad to see Angelique. She was the bright spot. She was the one person I believed could understand what I was going through. I could complain about Castlerock and she wouldn't try to persuade me how good it was for me like the adults would. She understood about missing my mom and even missing having parties. She got what it was like to have those nightmares. She got the frustration at being stuck here with all these kids that were so much worse than we were. She got it in a way the adults couldn't. She was my best friend.

So even though she had begun talking in a too-chipper voice, even though the backs of her hands were raw from washing and re-washing and her eyes seemed frantic, I was still happy to play whatever game she wanted. I had a friend in the world. I had that.

My mom started missing visits. She cancelled last minute saying her car was broken down or she had a last minute job interview. I knew she was probably drunk but I didn't say anything. I forgave her and pretended to myself that it was a car or a job and not her problems ruining my visits.

Staff would whine sweetly to me, "I'm so sorry." And: "Is there anything I can do?"

A flicker of a sneer would pass over me and I'd think of telling them all to fuck off or asking *what kind of wuss do you think I am?* But the look would be gone before it fully registered.

I'd answer, "It's no big deal. I'm fine. I'll catch her next time. These things happen." And smile.

Fall was passing. The real school year was under way and with it, fewer trips and more school projects. Friday Fun was a distant memory. Now there was only school work and treatment work and work and work and work.

My mom had canceled again and I went outside to rec with the other girls from Waterfalls. Angelique held my hand as we headed out.

"Boundaries, girls." Which meant no touching. She winked at me and we dropped hands.

The weather was extra warm and we tossed our jackets in a pile. We found a spot on a very small hilltop and I suggested we roll down the hill.

"I don't want to get my skirt dirty," she answered, looking down and smoothing her skirt.

She had court later that day. I was worried for her and wanted to make her feel better.

"Darn. It's a perfect hill for it." I shrugged. "Okay, what do you want to do?"

"Let's play babies. You be the baby and I'll be the mommy," she suggested.

"Okay."

Playing babies seemed to take her mind off her problems, so I sucked my thumb and talked in baby talk and asked for her to give me my bottle and put me down for a nap. She petted my hair and I lay back against the grass and watched massive puffs of clouds pass over us. I shivered and she got her shiny plastic pink coat out of the pile and laid it over me. I closed my eyes and pretended she was my mother. It was good to feel my mother close, even if it was just for pretend. I got to have her care and focus and love and it was all I'd ever dreamed of. When I closed my eyes like that, I pretended so hard, I smelled strawberries.

"*Boundaries*, girls."

The smell evaporated and I knew where we were and how weird it was. We went back to class.

It got so all Angelique wanted to play was babies anymore. I started to feel weird about it when she'd ask. I was worried about the way her hands had started scabbing and bleeding from all the washing. I knew it wasn't normal that she hadn't brushed her hair lately and I could see tiny scabs on her scalp from her picking at herself. Sometimes when she looked at me, it was like she wasn't in there. But I didn't say anything. She was my best friend and I just wanted someone to play with and to be normal.

Fall announced its impending departure with a distinct chill. Like a hint of Christmas oranges, it cut through the sunshine and into your nostrils with a tingle and left frost on the grass in the morning.

We were playing outside on the school lawn one day at lunch recess when Angelique lifted her shirt and showed me her stomach. All across her tiny, flat tummy were fingernail scratches. Jagged scabs in small arcs linked a line across her abdomen.

"It's my c-section scar, baby. It's the mark that shows where you came from. Now let Mama clamp and cut the cord so I can hold you."

And even though I should've gotten the staff and told them the whole truth, right then, I didn't want to hear about *boundaries*. I wanted to have someone pet my hair and tell me I was loved.

I wanted that someone to be my mom, of course. I wanted to smell her sweet strawberry scent and lay my head in her lap and be cared for and special.

But since my mom wasn't available, I let Angelique do it instead. And instead of oranges, I swore I smelled summer and strawberries as I drifted off.

16

The next day, my mom missed her visit. Car trouble, supposedly. Again.

I always got mad when we stood outside Science class waiting for the teacher. Attached to each class were observation rooms that were rarely used for observation. They were mostly filled with extra stuff the teachers shoved in there for storage. The hallway was wide, fifteen feet across with low-pile carpet and smooth painted drywall with sea foam green swirls painted on top of a soft cream color. It was supposed to be calming.

We had to stand along the wall outside the door, not touching, single file, with our hands folded in front of us or in our pockets. Technically we weren't supposed to talk either. I resented being told when to speak and what to do with my own hands. I wanted to talk to my friends between classes like normal middle school kids. I didn't want to do what I was told. And today, I really didn't want to do what I was supposed to.

I considered walking away. Leaving and not coming back. I pictured the long sidewalk where I walked with my mom. I'd step pointedly on all the cracks. A wicked smile snuck across my face at the thought and I wanted to punch someone just to feel my fist connect with soft doughy flesh.

"How're you, Seff?" I caught a glimpse of the art teacher's curly mass of hair bouncing toward her class.

My emotions jerked and changed directions. Suddenly, my spirits soared at seeing her, "Fine." I smiled. "Actually, great, Miss!"

She continued down the hall and I went back to leaning against the wall and waiting for the science teacher, who was always frazzled, always late, and always annoying.

Danny was standing against the wall talking to himself. He was chubby and dorky and had a jiggly belly that he got teased for. He had his three things, as usual. He *had* to have those three things. His eraser and silly putty were tucked up under his arm so he could hold his teddy to his face and talk to it.

"We wewe on yellow yestewday, teddy, becawse of you. You can't wandew off wike that. Stay here wif me so we do bettew today."

He nodded once and kissed the bear on the nose.

He usually didn't bother me much but today he was so annoying. I thought about all the things the kids disliked about him. He was uncoordinated and always on the losing team of every PE class. But even though he'd lose, he'd pump his fist in the air on the way down the hall and tell everyone how awesome he was at dodge ball or whatever sport we were playing. When we had inside recess and played board games, he always lost but would complain it was because the rules were unfair. When kids did better than him at anything he always had some excuse why.

I was usually nice to him because he was one of the unadoptables. No one seemed to know what happened to his parents, just that he didn't have any and that he had matching scarred-up palms that looked like they'd been burned really badly. We knew when scars matched like that, they came from a kid's parents. So, even though he got on my nerves, I pitied him enough that I usually left him alone.

Angelique, on the other hand, was completely unsympathetic to Danny. She never liked him and was always snotty to him. But with him in our academic group, she was even more vicious. She didn't like him traveling from class to class with our academic group. His cottage had gotten a bunch of new kids at once and was in upheaval. He'd lost it with his own group and been coming with us to try to give his class a break from him or him from them or something while the group worked out the pecking order. So he was with us, messing up our classes.

Angelique called him retarded and hated the way the whole class had to wait for the teacher to explain a separate lesson to him because he couldn't handle the work we did. Even though she called him retard and mongoloid, Danny had a crush on Angelique.

I slouched against the wall with my fingers laced and my hands where they were supposed to be. But I scooted a few inches closer to Angelique and nudged her with my elbow, nodding my head toward Danny.

I whispered in baby talk, "Mommy, that boy was mean to me. He took my teddy bear."

She smiled. "My poor, poor baby. No one treats my baby like that. I'll get it back for you. Don't you worry."

My emotions bounced around all class period. At one point, I'd want to go draw in the art room and I'd feel good picturing the names project I'd been helping with. But then I felt like jumping out of my seat and going for a long run, screaming at the top of my lungs, and I hated everyone in the room and wanted to make them pay for that hatred.

I scratched my nails into the wood of the desk, feeling the waxy surface give way under my nail. I felt it sink further until my nail reached the wood beneath. I pressed on and the wood splintered into the tender skin in my nail bed. The pain felt good. I wanted a drink. I wanted to let the amber liquid warm and numb me from the inside out. I wanted to carve all the names into the underside of a table.

I didn't want to feel good. I didn't want to feel. I wanted to kick a gray dog.

Finally class let out and we walked down the hall in a single file line. I unlaced my fingers and swung my arms.

"Boundaries!" a staff member yelled at me, but I pretended not to hear. Staff walked away for a minute and left us in front of the lunchroom.

I leaned against the carpeted curved wall. We stood in line like usual and my anger itched. I glared.

"Is my baby still sad about her teddy?" Angelique coaxed.

My eyes went wide and sad and I pouted and nodded slowly.

There were small streaks of dried blood across the back of her hand where she'd wiped blood after picking at her scabs. She sidled her tiny frame up to Danny and smiled into his face.

The look that passed over his face first of shock and then absolute bliss was unforgettable. She kissed him on the cheek then got an evil grin as she tugged the teddy away from him. "Don't you take my baby's teddy, you *retard*."

Danny was beside himself. He liked Angelique. But he *needed* the three things. He went wild. He started swinging and throwing his weight around. He was like a bowling ball, knocking into whichever kid was next to him and leaving behind wreckage. I looked into Angelique's face.

She was smiling. Her smile stood strong against the torrent of fighting. She was the eye of the storm and she was happy about it.

Staff came running. The hallway became pandemonium. There was a call over the loud speaker for "structural support" (code for restraints).

There were restraints left and right. The new kids who hadn't seen this before, who didn't know how to get out of the way, rioted. They began hitting staff who were on the ground. This led to more restraints.

The problem with that many restraints at the same time is that none of the kids can calm down in front of all the other kids. They're worried about saving face, or they're already amped up and the kid next to them is screaming "nigger" or "spic" which keeps them going and going. And the staff are afraid to let go. It's really likely if you let one of those kids go, they'll kick the kid who said "spade" in the face while he's held down by the adults.

I calmed briefly when the art teacher looked into my face and said, "Seffra, you're better than this. And you're going to make the right decision if I have to carry you out of here myself, so help me God."

She was no joke and it focused me and I believed her. I started to leave with her when I heard someone yell "Baby Killer!"

The teacher turned to see, and I, convinced in my confusion that the staff restraining her had said this, attacked. I went up and reached to slap her in the face when hands grabbed me and I was on the ground. I don't know how they did it so fast.

I'm not sure how Francie got there, but I heard her say, "Breathe, just breathe."

The adults above me took deep breaths and my breathing matched theirs in moments. I snapped out of my adrenaline-filled mania but I couldn't stop picturing the smile on Angelique's face.

Even in the chaos of all that screaming and swearing, all I could contemplate was Angelique's placid, frozen smile.

My restraint was brief. They let me loose and I went to my home-room where they got a lunch for me. I swallowed mushy green beans whole, not bothering to chew since it was basically the consistency of baby food anyway. I stared into nowhere and wondered where Angelique had gone and why she was smiling when she'd left me and Danny's teddy behind.

The chaos continued for what felt like hours. The calm kids were taken to their homerooms and then we were all quietly brought back to our cottages and the cottages were put on "slow down."

"Slow down" meant being on near constant silence and staying in our cottages all the time. No one talked unless we were doing groups and we did nothing but groups and room time for that day and the next.

During these groups, if you refused to do something or were "noncompliant" in any way, you were either restrained or put in the time-out room. We had lots of room time and lots of worksheets and "accountability."

At first, I didn't take any accountability. This was just how Castlerock was. It was a fucked up place full of fucked up kids and so fucked up stuff like riots happened. That wasn't my fault. It just was.

But then I thought of Ang's smile. I thought of how I should've said something. I thought of how weird her smile had gotten and all the warnings I'd ignored.

First thing the next morning, Horatio was in our cottage with his usual energy. "What does anger feel like?" he hollered.

I pictured scratching my back against the gray wall carpet outside the cafeteria. I'd been so mad, a type of mad that was sinister and rotten.

"It itches until it bursts," I said.

Danny was overweight, as I've said before. He had a roly-poly belly. He needed his three things.

I almost didn't interrupt Horatio's excited sermon about anger and how it bursts. I thought of Angelique as my mom and the smile before she checked out. I felt the rot of her smile falling apart before my eyes and how I could have stopped it all if I'd just said something about Angelique instead of letting my own anger out on Danny. I'd just wanted someone to take care of me so badly and I was so angry. It felt good to let it out on Danny, to release my crazy "mom" Angelique on him. But if I had told someone about Angelique and stayed away from her, we wouldn't be here on slow down.

"I'm ready to give my accountability. I told Angelique that Danny took my teddy. She took it from him and that started the whole thing."

As I said, on slow down we had a lot of room time. But this was an abnormal amount of room time. Waterfalls was an eerie level of quiet. It was the quiet of wreckage settling and inventory being taken before decision and action. I tried to read but I waited in the calm. I was curious. I knew it had turned riotous but that had happened before. Maybe not quite this badly, but it wasn't unheard of. But missing school to stay in the cottages on slow down was new.

There were whispers from staff and the phone kept ringing. Caseworkers. *Seffra? She's fine. But yes, this does happen. Especially to obese children. Yes, she was restrained. No, she's fine now.*

I pictured Danny on his belly the day before.

I'd looked over my shoulder as I was being led away.

"I can't bweeve," he'd been yelling, his brown eyes shown with strain. His teddy was on the floor in the middle of the hallway. It was dirty from being stepped on and held so tightly.

I walked on, Francie's hand on my shoulder guiding me. We all said we couldn't breathe when we were restrained. But the look on his face stuck with me.

Staff wasn't trying to hurt him, I really believe that. But in the adrenaline of all those restraints and all that yelling, maybe staff put too much weight on him, or stayed on him for too long.

He took a nap. There were whispers about it and word made it to me. *They couldn't wake him up.*

I lay in my bed hoping he'd fallen asleep with those three things. I hoped they'd let him pick up his teddy when his restraint was over. Tears I never wiped away dripped into my ears and I heard watery words, phrases of *it's so sad, no parents to notify. Those? Those were scars from his parents burning his hands on the stove when he was a baby.* And I wished I could melt underwater and not hear that I'd killed again.

17

With Danny dead, there was an investigation. Social workers and therapists interviewed the kids about what happened before the riots and during. Francie pulled me from groups first thing in the morning.

I was honest. But who knows what I said, what I remembered. I admitted that I'd picked on Danny. I confessed about Angelique picking at herself and washing her hands until they bled. I told Francie about playing babies. I told her about asking Ang to take Danny's teddy bear. I told her it was my fault he was dead. I told her I could take accountability. I could.

She listened and didn't say much. She said she'd want to talk more with me later but that for now I needed to relax. She made a call and there was a new pill at med passing.

While I was talking to Francie, Angelique's caseworker met with her. Angelique wasn't at the cottage when I got back.

"Where is she?" I asked the Mouseketeers.

"We can't tell you that because of confidentiality," was all they'd tell me, while they packed up her stuff and shoved it in shiny black trash bags that they left by the front door with her name taped to the pile.

Her picking at herself was one of the signs she was headed downhill. It wasn't the first time this had happened with her. It wasn't even the first time she got another girl to play babies with her. Francie told me. She wasn't supposed to but she did. It didn't matter. Ang was gone before she was kicked out of Castlerock. Her mind was gone; you could see it in her eyes.

I never saw her again. I could've helped. Instead I'd played babies. I took the extra pill and slept.

18

One time a group of kids ran together. It was early in the fall. They were gone overnight. Met up with some older kids and partied all night. A girl had sex with an older guy at the party. They all got high. The police were called. Their stuff got packed up and they were sent on their way afterwards.

When I first got to Castlerock, before I was hospitalized, before I knew that your stuff could get packed up and you could get kicked out, I ran one time. I wasn't trying to party or get kicked out.

At the time, I didn't know that was a possibility. I just wanted to feel my legs move. Normally when I "ran" I threw up a middle finger and left the room. They called that running but I don't agree. Those were breaks. I peeked in other classrooms and watched what they were doing. I sat in the stairwell. I went to the chill room and kicked the wall, screamed for a while, or sat on the concrete floor and felt the quiet echo of my voice vibrating against the hollow walls.

That time, I ran and ran until my legs tired out and the rubbery tingle slowed me. Then, I walked on the white concrete suburban sidewalks. They were newly-poured like the slabs on the Hill, the orderly little Italian neighborhood in St. Louis. But the sidewalks here were wider, somehow newer, better. The Zoysia grass lay thick like a lustrous carpet next to me. No dandelions. Nothing out of place.

I walked around and smiled at people out walking their dogs. I wished I could feel something other than fury at them for everything they had. Even the cracks in their sidewalks were planned and regular, orderly. I resented everything about those people, normally.

But this time, while on the run, I stood still moment considering my options. I looked at the white rubber on my sneakers and reached a toe over the line, testing the grass under my foot. But then instead, I pulled my foot back and kept walking. The tingle in my legs calmed me and instead of hating them, I decided to be one of them. I walked along smiling and occasionally scratching behind the ears of a poodle, asking in that chipper voice I'd not yet gotten used to, "Aw, what's his name?"

I pretended to be visiting my aunt and uncle for the week. I was in from Georgia. I remarked on the weather and the lovely parks. My belly felt full and my wrists were loose and calm. I pretended normal and I liked it.

"Seffra, the reason we're here is because we care about you and we have to talk to you."

I felt swimmy. The new drug was heavy in my arms and back and I felt drunk. I was sitting in Francie's office with Francie and Alison and Horatio. I thought I was in trouble. I remember thinking that I didn't want to get moved like Angelique had and being angry with her, even though what happened was as much my fault as hers.

"Listen, I promise I'm trying. I didn't mean to get restrained. I'm going to do better. I really, really am."

Horatio put a hand firmly on my leg for a moment and then took it back and rubbed between his eyes.

"I know I should have told someone about Angelique. I'm really trying though."

"It's not that." Alison spoke. "Seffra, there's no easy way to tell you this…" She faltered and tripped over her words for a second. "Your mother relapsed. She was found by the police a few days ago, but it took some time to be sure it was her."

To be sure it was her echoed in my head.

I thought of that grass, how I wanted to lay in it and not talk about what they wanted to talk about. How much I didn't want the snowstorm that was on its way. How much the idea of Christmas made me want to break and ruin things. I just wanted the grass and strawberries and to feel my lungs fill up with water.

"She was in a coma for about a day but she didn't make it. I'm sorry."

She didn't make it.

"What do you mean you're sorry? Why?"

Horatio had his hands folded in front of his face and seemed to be praying.

"Why are you sorry?"

I saw behind his hands; he had tears in his eyes.

Francie spoke softly. "Seffra, Alison is trying to tell you that your mother died. That's why she's sorry. We're all so sorry to have to tell you this."

Died?

I turned my head slowly from person to person. Time seemed to provide extra keen detail but through a filter of tingles and water in my ears. I stared at the people in the room.

Alison was dressed up. Her brow was knit ever so slightly and her blonde hair was pulled back neatly in a bun. She was wearing expensive black slacks and a white button down shirt. She looked like she should carry a violin.

Horatio wore a gray t-shirt and jeans. He had a red flannel shirt tied around his waist. You could see the bulk of his thickly muscled legs against his light blue jeans. His leg jiggled a little but he just kept whispering a prayer with his eyes closed and his head bent over.

I looked at Francie last. She sniffled and wiped a tear from her eye. But something was off and I couldn't think about her tears because something wasn't right. I kept thinking something was different about her. Her eyes. The look in her eyes, was that it? No. She looked different.

"You got contacts," was all I said.

19

They talked about putting me in the hospital or keeping me under a close watch: one-to-one they call it, meaning you have a staff member assigned to you. They tried to ask me what I wanted but all I wanted was to lie in the grass. Could you make a Zoysia-angel in December? On the walk I'd taken, you could. I knew, you just had to believe it and you could. It was like Christmas and Santa.

I wished Angelique hadn't checked out. I thought of the absent look in her eyes and was sad. I wished she hadn't been sent away. I wished I could be her baby, even with her yucky scabs, and I could lie back in the grass while she told me, "Mommy will make sure nobody hurts you." I wished I could drink whiskey and wave my arms up and down in the grass while she talked to me. I put my thumb in my mouth and let them decide.

The team settled on one-on-one. I'd done well in the hospital in the past, but Alison reminded them that she'd have to look for a foster placement and so she wanted fewer hospitalizations on the books. If we could avoid one, so much the better for finding me a home in the future. Horatio wanted to be one of the ones to stay with me and I nodded that was okay with me. I didn't care.

Well, I cared a little. I didn't want a Mouseketeer. The art teacher and Horatio were definitely better than the Mouseketeers any day.

The next few days after I found out my mom was dead went by in a blur. There were moments that were so vivid they were almost florescent. They couldn't be real; they were too real.

There were times I washed my hands for long periods. The water went on and on in that Barbie-pink basin. Water splashed and sliced its chill into my bones and I both begged it to cut into my skin, to slice me apart with ice, at the same time as I ignored its frigidity and let it pour on while I waited far away. When I was finished, I avoided the reflection of my own face in the mirror because I didn't want anything to be that real.

Other whole sections of time seemed to disappear.

I remember going for walks with Horatio and him praying, praying all the time, muttering, "Our Father, Who art in heaven, hallowed be Thy name," again and again. He whispered prayers and every once in a while looked up and told me, "I'm here for you."

I couldn't feel my legs.

I remember my cold hands against my face as I sat with Horatio at the table in the cottage. I watched him sop up mashed potatoes and gravy with a roll but then never take the bite. I liked the slick lines across the white plate. I wished the roll were gone and the plate were clean.

Why wouldn't he take the bite?

I threw my food away untouched.

Then there was this moment when I snapped to. I didn't just want out of Castleock like I had before. It wasn't the simple human desire to run away. It was the moment the world clicked into place and the absolute truth of realization struck in one single location at one instant like lightening. I knew I had to change. Something had to be different. I needed out because things had to change and be different or

I'd destroy myself. I'd become like lightening and burn myself up if I didn't do something. I needed to make do. I needed to grow a new ring. I suddenly needed to talk to Francie or Alison or whoever. Right. Then.

Francie was keeping her schedule as open for me as she could. So a call from the cottage was all it took to get me in to see her. I walked up to her door and knocked.

"Come in."

She looked like the regular Francie. Dark hair, loosely pulled back with pieces coming free and falling around her face. She always looked a little disheveled. She picked her glasses up and slid them on.

"What's up?"

"I have to get out of here." I stood there.

"Okay? Uh…" She gestured toward my usual spot, but I didn't sit.

I paced while I explained why I'd come. "I have to get out of here as soon as possible. I can't stay here. I can't be where Danny died and where I used to visit my mom and cat McDonald's and shit. I can't be where I didn't help Ang. I can't be here. I'm getting worse here. I learn worse shit to do. Listen to me; I even swear more. I'm going to make worse friends. I have to get out. Please, you have to help me."

She nodded. "I know you've always said no to living with a foster family. I don't know if this idea is even a possibility right now, I'm only asking this question to see how you feel about it. So would you go to a foster home now?"

I sat down finally. "Yes. Whatever it takes. Get me out of here."

She nodded and slid her glasses down. There was a soft light thud as her glasses hit the pad of paper in her lap. "I'm so glad you came and talked to me. I really am. It shows a lot of growth, that you can voice what you want and be clear about why. I'm going to need to think about what you've said a little more, Seffra. No promises, but I'm proud of you for coming to me." No promises.

As soon as she was done speaking, I stood back up and was halfway out the door when she said, "One more thing." I didn't turn back. "It's likely you'll still be here for a little bit at least. Even if you're not, you might be surprised to find when you leave that there are things you miss about Castlerock. If you were leaving tomorrow, what would you say were the best parts?"

I nodded. "Okay, but I still need to get out of here."

I added another "please" before I left.

20

I was still on one-to-one and they'd pulled a random night worker I didn't know from one of the other cottages to hang out with me. She was pale and skinny and had long dark hair she wore in a ponytail. She reminded me of a rat tossed into the sun.

I'd convinced her that I needed some time to myself and she'd agreed to let me read in my room alone. I had spent my entire life wanting my mother. Wanting her to pay bills, buy food, be nice to me, take care of me, sing and dance with me, play with me, pay attention to me. Without my mom, I didn't know what to want.

I kept thinking of how I'd felt that day I'd run. When I was walking through the neighborhood pretending to be visiting from out of town, I felt great. I felt light and like none of my past was part of the conversation. It was a breeze.

I could do the same in foster care. I could leave all this behind. Leave it in the wood of the bunk beds. Leave it in the hollow walls. Leave it in the restraints and the bullshit rules. I could walk away and live with some perfect family who'd let me scratch behind the ears of their dog and feed me good meals. It could be easy.

I knew Francie would ask about the best parts stuff before she told me anything in our next session, so I really did think about what I liked at Castlerock. At first, I just rehearsed answers. I liked the food. I liked my bed and knowing I could eat as much as I wanted. The rehearsed answers led to more answers. I liked the art teacher and I liked Horatio. It occurred to me that I wouldn't see them after I left.

I thought of a day when Horatio had led group. It was Team Building and Leadership group, which I'd really liked because Horatio ran it.

We walked into our classroom to see that all the desks and chairs had been moved to the side. There was a carpet in the middle of the room that the desks usually framed in. It had squares in rows with each color of the rainbow going horizontally across. It looked brighter without all the desks around it. Horatio sat on the prep table at the front of the room and enthusiastically waved his arm.

"Welcome, come in!"

We looked around, curiously skeptical. "What's going on?"

"Nothin'. How're you today?" He stuck out his lip and shrugged as if to say, *what are you talking about?*

"Why's the room all crazy?" we tried again.

"Oh, you'll see once everyone's here."

"You two together," he motioned. "And you, you're with Seffra." He paired me with a kid I'd never even sat next to.

I pursed my lips and raised an eyebrow. *What kinda bullshit is this?*

I wasn't the only one.

"I don't want to be with him. We don't get along," one kid complained.

Horatio ignored us and tied a blindfold on the kid. Horatio winked at the rest of us and held a finger up to his lips while tossing objects all over the floor: pillows, books, tipped-over chairs and desks. There were things strewn everywhere. He smiled.

"Okay, now lead your partner across the carpet. But if he makes one wrong step, he's done. BOOM." The *b* burst from his lips and he beamed.

The object of the game was to talk to your partner and give careful instructions for how to cross without hitting a "landmine." If you touched any of the objects on the ground, you were dead and would have to wait your turn to try again. The person crossing had to listen carefully because the stuff was dropped on the floor while they were blindfolded.

The first team that went didn't make it. A skinny pimple-faced boy gave a tall, red-head directions.

"Take two steps to the right."

The redhead stepped on a landmine.

"I told you two steps; you took two *giant* steps. If I'd known you were going to take such big steps, I would have only told you one."

"It's not my fault, *you* told me two steps. I have long legs."

"Eh, next," Horatio said and blindfolded another kid.

When the next group also stepped on a landmine, they got even madder. He interrupted, "Boys and girls, this is what it's all about. To be good leaders, you have to communicate well. You have to give good instructions, and you have to work together and get to know each other."

"Next team."

He blindfolded the next kid and rearranged the objects on the floor. The next team made it almost the entire way. Again there was squabbling. The next two teams made it across.

Then it was my team. For our turn, I was blindfolded and my partner gave the instructions.

"Two baby steps left. Actually one more. Lift your right foot up, higher. Ok, now there's a pile of text books. I want you to step over them."

"Look out for that big desk!" exclaimed Horatio.

I faltered and tripped. My foot landed on the books and he said "Boom! You hit a mine. Sorry guys."

"What the hell, I mean heck?" I said, pulling the blindfold off. "You told me to watch out. You messed us up on purpose."

"Ah, but I said the only person you were supposed to listen to was your partner."

"Fine, let me have another turn then."

He shook his head. I was mad. I knew I could do it. I needed another try now that I knew how it worked.

All the teams took lots more turns. We switched to giving directions and leading our partners then we took turns being led again and the rest of the class were allowed to attempt to distract the blindfolded kid. You had to focus in on your partner's voice and block everything else out.

When it was my turn again, Horatio threw a pillow at me.

It hit me in the belly but I didn't even flinch. I smiled. "Man, you think you can stop me with some ol' pillow?"

I kept focused on my partner and kept going and as I crossed, Horatio clapped two pillows on either side of me and nearly knocked me over.

"You think you can make it all easy, girl?" he teased.

I smugly pulled the blindfold off and stuck my tongue out at him. "I told you, you can't stop me with that ol' pillow!" I'd made it across. I pumped my fist.

We all laughed. It was a really fun group.

At the end of it all, Horatio sat us down in a circle and asked us what we thought the landmines were.

"Bombs," someone said.

Kids adjusted their positions on the floor. What had just been a group of us sitting crisscross-applesauce was now a misshapen group of half-lounging kids.

"Yes, that's true, but in life, what are the landmines that you can hit, what things will stop you from getting through, what will blow you up?"

"Drugs!" someone said. Several of the kids who had been laying down, sat up now. Hands went up.

"Yes, what else?" Horatio called on a kid.

"Poor choices." More kids sat up.

"Be more specific." He pointed at someone else.

"Spray painting someone's house."

"Gangs!" came the answers.

Kids sat up on their knees now barely able to stay seated at all.

He held up his hands and gently motioned with both hands to quiet us. "Now, how do you get through these things? Can you always see them coming?"

"No, you can't see them coming. Plenty of things can mess up your life and they'll come out of nowhere," I said. I was standing now.

"But you can see them sometimes, right?" Horatio gestured for me to sit and I did.

"Well, yeah." I answered.

"In group today, how did we avoid them?"

"We listened to advice from our partners."

"Was that advice always good?"

"No."

What he was getting at hit me. Heads all around the room nodded to what he said. We were back to closely resembling a circle of seated kids. "There are bad influences and bad leaders that will try to lead you toward drugs and gangs and all kinds of things that aren't really going to help you. You have to pick out the good voices to listen to."

Now, with my mom dead, I heard Horatio's voice. It was only a whisper and it was praying. He prayed because he didn't know where to lead me. I listened. "Our Father, Who art in Heaven." I didn't know what that meant; my father was in jail.

I remembered another group with Horatio. I'd been mad. Steaming mad. Piping mad. And it was Anger Management group.

He asked us to come up with an animal to represent us when we're angry. People said they were lions and hippos and all kinds of things. Then they got to me.

At my turn I said, "I'm a gas can. The liquid ignites and it won't stop until it burns out, it spills on other people and burns them alive."

No one said anything for a moment, then some dipshit said, "That's not an animal." I glared and was about to say *man, fuck you.*

But then Horatio said, "No, that's okay. So what if it's not an animal. That's excellent, Seffra! Really good image."

Then he asked us to come up with strengths for our anger, what was good about the animals we'd all picked. We went around in a circle. Everyone would have to go. Lions were strong and proud and blah, blah, blah. What should I say? That kid was right, mine wasn't an animal.

I thought and I thought and the whole room was quiet, held back by the patience of Horatio. "Take your time. Take as much time as you need. What strength is there in your image of your anger?" He repeated the question slowly and I turned it over in my mind.

"I guess you could use it to cook animals if you didn't have a camp fire. You could use it to feed yourself and keep you warm, I mean if you didn't have anything else," I said, unsure of myself. Before anyone could mock me though, Horatio came in.

"*Exactly*! Whew!" Horatio said, clapping his hands together and hopping off the end of the desk he was sitting on, pointing at me. "You get it! The thing is, your anger *can* be useful. It *can* keep you warm, it *can* keep you fed when there's nothing else."

He suddenly turned to the other students and began pointing at them. "But what happens when that anger runs out? What happens if you don't add more things to your life than just your anger?" He turned back to me for an answer. Horatio was a preacher on the weekends and you could see why: he was good; I was captivated. He was right, my anger kept me able to sustain myself, but it wouldn't work forever, unless I continued adding fuel to the gas can.

"Well, when you burn off all the gas, eventually you're lonely and cold. So I guess what you're saying is I should use my anger, but I should have other things to help me too."

That's what he'd wanted us to get out of the group. Our anger was a tool, a profound revelation and probably a controversial stance at a treatment center full of angry kids.

But anger couldn't be our only tool to deal with the world. We'd need others. We'd need coping skills. These were other institutional words, but they meant what they sounded like and were useful. I needed to add more than a gas can and a Swiss army knife to my tool belt.

I wished Horatio could be one of my tools. He helped me. I knew I could pick his enthusiastic voice out in a crowd. I knew my anger could be useful because of him. I would miss him. I could honestly report back to Francie. I would miss Horatio.

But it was more than that too. I spent all this time trying to figure out how to be with my mom. Scheming how to run away to her, being good to get home, fantasizing about my perfect life with her. I spent all this time hating Castlerock and wanting to be with her. And now when I thought back on it, I'd learned a lot.

I'd learned how to *be* without her. I'd learned from living with her that I could take care of myself. And I'd learned from Castlerock how to figure out all the rules and how to get through it. I'd learned about my anger and my body and my emotions. I knew I could do it when I got to foster care. I'd miss Horatio, but I could do it.

21

It was almost bedtime and they were passing meds. I was on green so I'd get to stay up late, but I still took my meds at the same time as everyone else. The new blue pill sat in its small Dixie cup; it promised the numb, easy sleep that made me wake newly drunk and lost each morning. But I had tools. I had anger and I had a whispering voice praying. I listened.

"I don't mean to be rude or nothin' but do I have to take the blue one? It makes me feel kinda, I don't know… not good."

"You always have the right to refuse your meds. I'll have to note it and give your therapist a call though." There was a tone of warning, nearing a threat. Giving your therapist a call sounded like something that got documented and meant you weren't ready to move on.

I thought about this. "What if *I* called my therapist? Could I do that?" I was nervous that the worker would think I was being a pain and knock me off green for it, but I wanted to see how I felt without that pill. The pill was a watery cheat. I could slog along with it, but I thought my foster family would notice I was wasted and that could be a problem. If I could even get a foster family…

She shrugged. "You have to call the therapist on call."

"That's okay."

I took the pill then but the next time I met with Francie, I had a list of things to ask about including not taking that pill anymore.

※

"Seffra, I'm surprised to see you so, so..." She faltered.

"Together?"

"Yeah. Honestly, I thought you'd take the news of your mother harder than this. Can you tell me about that?"

I shrugged. "I guess it doesn't really feel real, you know? I mean, I miss her. But I'm used to missing her. I've been missing her my whole life." I shrugged again. "So I have a list of stuff to talk to you about," I continued.

She raised her eyebrows.

"First, my meds."

She agreed to get a med appointment for me and assured me that the staff's not allowed to consequence me for refusing meds. I said I was going to see how I felt without it and tell the doctor at the med appointment.

"Okay, foster care. You said I have to tell you about what I'll miss about this place. At first, I thought that was a weird thing to ask and didn't think I'd miss anything. But then..."

I gave the report I'd thought up about the things I'd miss about Castlerock. I even told her that at first I'd only thought of stuff like the food and my bedspread but that then I'd really thought about Horatio. I confessed that I'd miss Angelique too even though I knew she was a voice that steered me toward landmines. She'd been a friend and despite what that prick Dante said to me, I *did* remember who my friends were.

Still, I didn't want to end up like Ang. I didn't want scars and scabs and to age-out. I wanted to walk away cleaner, better, tougher, healed. I said so. "I want to live in a foster home."

"Well then, we've got some work to do."

There were things I'd have to do. I had to stay on green. I couldn't run or get restrained. I had to really do my treatment work. But if I played the game, if I followed their rules, I could get out. It was like the group Horatio had led with the landmines. I knew how it worked now. I knew how to get around. I could get across.

I worked my butt off for the next couple months. I kept my nose down. I didn't talk to the other kids much. I made arrangements to leave if I wanted to go for a walk and sometimes Francie let me earn walks during our sessions. She upped our sessions to twice a week to help get me out. It meant something to Alison that she did that.

The next time I saw Alison for our monthly face-to-face contact, she came to Castlerock to have a meeting. It was just before Christmas.

Horatio was there and so was Francie. The adults talked for a while and then they brought me in.

"The team tells me you're determined to make it in foster care. Is that true?" Alison asked.

I nodded.

Horatio winked at me. "If this girl was leading a revolution, I'd follow her. She'd lead us all. She'd be *that* determined."

I covered my smile and my face flushed deeply.

"If you and your team are willing to work this hard to get you out of here, I'm willing to work just as hard to find you a foster family."

I prayed at night that Uncle Phin would help me. I was mad at him because I blamed him for not watching out for my mom. I blamed him for letting her die. *Where were you, you asshole? Why didn't you help? Now you owe me.*

I wasn't sure about God. I just didn't know. So I kept talking to Uncle Phin. *I'm afraid of not getting a family. And what if I do? I'm afraid of a foster family too. What if I don't like them? What if they don't like me?*

Oh my god, what if they're like the Crosbys?

I listened but time was my only answer. I had to wait.

Then I met with Alison. She assured me that she'd keep meeting with me to make sure there was a good fit with the family. She wouldn't disappear on me. She'd see it through. I pictured the day I'd run and pretended to be in from Georgia visiting relatives. I hoped it would be like that. I resolved to leave behind what I could and move on with all the tools they'd given me.

Christmas was complete bullshit and that strengthened my resolve. Volunteers we'd never heard from before or since came out of the woodwork to *give back*. There were presents on top of presents and hot chocolate and Santa. A senator came to visit and take pictures with us. It was faker than the tinsel decorations with snow from an air can.

I let a layer of myself die. Or maybe not die but go dormant, flatten. I let myself set my sights on a new ring, a new life. And I knew I could do it. I knew I could make it through anything. I could sprout something new. I could figure out any rules or routines. I could make do if I needed to. I always had. Whether my mom was there or not, I'd always been able to make do.

Just after Christmas, I packed up my things, said goodbye to Horatio and the art teacher, and I went to live with a foster family. I followed the life I was given and made do.

If you cut into my skin, right then, there would be a new ring just beginning. There would be sap and sinew, and life: green and filled with uncertainty and future and possibility...

DISCUSSION GUIDE

- Who is Seffra Morgan? What does she look like and what is her personality like?
- Suicide has touched many of us and is a topic worthy of serious discussion. How has it touched your life? What could you do if you were concerned that someone you care about might commit suicide? If you've considered suicide, how might you make a different choice than to act on that desire? What ways could you go about asking for help and why have you or have you not sought them out? Share a time when you asked for help and what the outcome was.
- Who is to blame for the bullying Seffra goes through at school?
- This book takes place in the early 1990s. How might the book be different if it took place today? How could you tell it took place in the 90s?
- Why might Seffra have tried to blend in and go without being noticed or "unexist" instead of standing up for herself or fighting back?
- What character stands out the most to you and why? If you could talk to that person, what might you say?
- What help is out there for kids like Seffra? In your perfect world, what help *would* be out there for her and kids like her?
- Describe Seffra's relationship with her mother: the good, the bad, and the ugly. Why do you think the author chose to show this type of relationship?
- Does Seffra believe literally that Uncle Phin is her guardian angel? Why does she talk to him?
- Seffra believes, as many kids in her situation do, that she at least partially deserves the sexual abuse and other poor treatment she receives. The nature of abuse is such that children must believe to some degree that they are in control of the

abuse. It is a survival tactic. Seffra believed "there was something wrong with me, something without a name. Something that made me look dirty and available to men." Beyond the survival rationale for why Seffra feels this way, what things in our culture might lead her to believe she deserved this treatment?

- Sexual development is more complicated than we are led to believe. What do you think the sexual behavior between Seffra and Kara means for Seffra's life? Why does it happen? What will she think about it when she gets older?

- What do you think would be the biggest hurdle to overcoming Seffra's life up to the point of entering Castlerock? How might you suggest she overcome that hurdle? Did she overcome it the way you thought she would? What will be her biggest hurdle moving forward?

- Why do you think Seffra and Angelique developed a friendship? Their play was meant to reflect something about the central problem to their lives, what was the central problem for each of them?

- Why did Danny really need the 3 things? Why do you think kids in the institution were restrained? Could they "control their own bodies?"

- Seffra's emotions jump around a lot in the second part of the book. Why do you think this is? What emotion dominates?

- If you could design the perfect person to work at a residential treatment facility/institution for children, what traits would that person possess? What do you think children in these facilities need?

- The author talks about the "unadoptables" who will "age-out." What should be done to support these kids who still age-out today?

- Do you think Seffra believes in God?